IF I'M LOST, HOW
COME I FOUND YOU?

IF I'M LOST, HOW COME I FOUND YOU?

by WALTER OLEKSY

cover by Leonard Shortall

SCHOLASTIC BOOK SERVICES
New York Toronto London Auckland Sydney Tokyo

To Ann, Donna, Katie and Tom Dillman,
Nora O'Callaghan, Laure, Mudd, Betsy,
Carolyn, and Tom Coyne,
Charlie and Chelsea.

ISBN 0-590-12095-6

14 13 12 11 10 9 8 7 6 5 4   1 2 3 4 5 7 6/8

Printed in the U.S.A.   06

Contents

FUN AND GAMES

Quacky stood, short and lean, slouched and fidgeting, in front of a desk in a small office. A tall, thin lady was seated behind it, filling out an official form on him. She had a nose, he thought, long as a pickle.

He shifted his weight from one foot to the other, looking around the room and rejecting it. It was a typical dumb office. Not worth staying in five minutes. He didn't intend being there any longer than that.

He wore the only clothes he liked to wear: old, frayed blue jeans without a belt and a light blue football jersey a size too big, with the large blue numerals "38" across the chest. His track shoes were taped together so they wouldn't fall apart, and he wore no socks. His ankles were dirty, but he didn't care.

The lady stared up into Quacky's small face with its bright blue eyes and at his long straight blond hair, which needed washing and cutting. She seemed puzzled.

"Age?" she asked.

"I'd say about fifty," he replied, switching his weight again.

"No games, young man," she snapped impatiently. "You know what I mean."

"Oh, you mean *my* age!" Quacky looked at her innocently. "Going on sixteen."

"In about four or five years," she said, flatly rejecting his arithmetic.

Quacky stopped looking around the office and saw her write down "12 plus" on his form. He didn't bother to correct her. He wasn't that sure of his age anyway. He knew he was an orphan, but that was about all he knew about himself. His parents had left him on the doorstep of a police station when he was only in diapers. He had been on his own ever since.

"Is Wilbur Quackenbush your real name?" she asked.

"It's the name I've been going by ever since I can remember. Except for short everyone calls me Quacky."

She shook her head and wrote the nickname down. She was on to his height and weight and Quacky came out about right this time. He always told people he was just a broom-handle wide and as tall as a cane.

"I have to get this form right!" the lady complained. "Can't you give me your height and weight in feet, inches, and pounds?"

"I'm not good at numbers," Quacky admitted. "You pick some."

She approximated his height and weight and wrote them down, grumbling.

Forms, schmorms, Quacky thought. Someone is always filling out forms on me. Sending me here. Moving me there. Always trying to keep track of me. He hated all the orphanages and foster homes they sent him to.

He knew what he wanted most of all. He wanted to be sent back to live in Smedley, Connecticut, with his Aunt Maggie. There he could raise pedigree dogs and make a lot of money.

But Aunt Maggie kept getting arrested for shoplifting. She took things because she didn't get enough money off her Social Security to live on. The state decided she was a bad influence on her nephew, so they took charge of Quacky.

"Do you know anything about your parents?" the lady asked.

"Pop was a movie star once, usually in Westerns," Quacky told her. "He always shot the bad guys and rode off into the sunset. Sometimes with the schoolteacher, sometimes with the mayor's daughter. But most of the time alone."

"Really? Your father was a movie star? What was his name?"

"If I knew that, I wouldn't be standing here," Quacky replied. "I'd be living in Hollywood now. Taking a dip in my swimming pool, with a hundred pedigree dogs around me."

She raised her pickle nose at him. "No need to make up stories about your parents," she said.

"Aren't you gonna ask me about my mother? Mom was a trapeze artist. She was the catcher. And a good one too!"

"Why is it you've moved around so much?" the lady asked. She didn't look as if she believed a word he said about either his father or mother.

"I keep reading my way through all the books in the libraries and orphanages and at the foster homes and get bored. I usually find some books at the next place that I haven't read. I stay until I've read everything, then I take off again."

"How did you leave the County Home for Boys and get here to New York City?" she asked.

Quacky began fidgeting more.

"Is there anything the matter, young man?"

"I have to go," Quacky replied.

"I'm sorry," she insisted, "but I'm not through with you yet."

"But I mean," he said firmly, "I've got to *go*!"

"Oh." She put down her pen. "There's a men's room just outside the door. Down the hall to the left. Be sure to come right back here afterward. We have to find a new home for you."

Quacky left the lady's office, closed the door behind him, and turned to the right. He walked casually out of the big old building and down about fifty stone steps to the sidewalk. The warm sun felt good outside.

From across the street he looked back at a sign over the entrance to the building from which he had just escaped. It read: NEW YORK HEADQUARTERS, COUNTY CORRECTIONAL HOME FOR LOST CHILDREN.

"Is *that* what they think I am . . . lost?" Quacky wondered out loud. People passing by paid no attention to him. "I know where I am . . . I'm here! I don't belong in there! I've never done anything that needed correcting."

Quacky suspected there were some who might argue about that, but no one at the moment was interested.

Without waiting for the lady inside the building to discover him missing and send police or bloodhounds after him, Quacky did what he was most used to doing. He ran.

He had never been in New York City before. It was so big, he wasn't sure it ever ended. It seemed to go on and on, street after street, row after row of tall buildings.

He didn't know exactly where to run next, but the farther away from the place he'd been the better.

After about a dozen blocks, he noticed a man in a fancy uniform staring at him. Quacky wondered if he might be a chief of police or someone else as important. If so, perhaps the man would arrest him and take him back to the lady, who would send him to another orphanage.

He had never seen a fancy hotel doorman before, so he had no way of knowing the man in the uniform was not a police chief. He just knew he had to get away from there.

Where could he hide? The answer became immediately apparent, across the street. He saw a neon sign flashing on and off: NCB Television Studios.

While the man in the fancy uniform was opening the door of a car, Quacky made a mad dash across the street.

So this is a television studio, he thought, standing in the gleaming lobby of NCB Television. It must be the biggest in the whole world!

"This way, Master Carlisle," he heard someone call out from behind him.

Turning around, Quacky saw a man in an orange-colored jumpsuit. He had a bushy black beard and mustache and a long, fat cigar.

"What's that?" Quacky asked. The man had grabbed Quacky firmly by an arm.

"You *are* Charles Q. Carlisle, the boy genius, aren't you?" the man said. "They said upstairs to expect some eccentric-looking boy. You certainly look and dress oddly enough. But you're almost late. You're due before the cameras in a couple of minutes. We just have time to get up to the seventieth-floor studio."

The man was pulling Quacky toward the elevators and Quacky decided to let him. He was being mistaken for a boy genius, apparently, and he wondered how he would like it. At least until they found out he wasn't one.

"Come into the private elevator." The man pushed Quacky in. "It's reserved for very special people. Where are your parents and your agent, by the way?"

"Oh, they got lost in traffic," Quacky improvised.

"Well, we can't wait for them. I'm the producer of *Mid-Day Fun and Games*, by the way. My name is Sebastian Damon. Welcome to TV Land."

Yukk, Quacky thought. A real strange bird. But at least it gets me away from all those men in uniform outside and the lady with a nose like a pickle.

The elevator stopped way up at the seventieth floor and Quacky felt dizzy. When the doors opened, and he and the man got out, he saw a huge studio full of television cameras. People were hurrying around like squirrels storing up nuts for winter. A band was blasting out some circus music, and so many lights were on, Quacky could hardly keep his eyes open.

"That outfit he's wearing . . . Impossible!" someone roared. "Wardrobe!"

A lady slapped Quacky in the face with a powder puff. The powder made him sneeze six times. He tried to tell her he had hay fever, but she ran off somewhere.

Someone else began painting his face. Then four men pulled him away, behind a curtain, and pulled his clothes off. They got him quickly into a white suit, a yellow shirt, a flowered tie, and white shoes.

"Two seconds to go!" someone called from the front side of the curtain. Quacky was dragged back onto the stage.

"One second!" a stagehand shouted.

"Go!"

Quacky waited with his mouth open. He was trying to keep from sneezing another six times — he always sneezed in sixes.

A man in a pink suit came magnificently from behind some striped curtains. Quacky saw a couple of hundred people sitting in seats in tiers going up practically to the ceiling. They began clapping and whistling and yelling. The band went into even louder circus music, and Quacky watched as the pink man came closer to him.

The man got bigger and fatter the closer

he came. By the time they were face to face, shaking hands, Quacky couldn't believe it.

"You're terribly overweight," Quacky told him. "Your ticker's going to give out. . . ."

The fat, pink man's face turned red and he began sputtering. Quacky wasn't sure if the man was having a heart attack or if he was just upset.

A moment later the man seemed to get hold of himself. He introduced himself as Uncle Pinky, as if Quacky should know him, he was so famous. But Quacky had watched only a little television at the orphanges and foster homes he had been to. He really preferred to read.

He had never watched *Mid-Day Fun and Games* or Uncle Pinky. He didn't know what to expect from either. But he decided that was okay. They wouldn't know what to expect from him either.

The band stopped playing and the audience quieted down. Uncle Pinky and Quacky sat on stools and Uncle Pinky explained about the show.

"Each day we have a new child guest who tries to win at our fun and games. Today the jackpot prize, if you win all the fun and games we put you through, is one thousand dollars."

"A thousand dollars?" Quacky was surprised at how low the figure was. "They give away more than that to the losers on most shows."

"What a wonderful sense of humor our guest has," Uncle Pinky said, squirming on his stool. "What would you do with a thousand dollars, if you won it?"

"I'd buy a couple of pedigree dogs and mate them," Quacky said. "Then I'd sell the pups for a couple hundred dollars apiece. Like my pal back home does. Ralph says he's gonna become a millionaire with Clemontis Regis."

"And who or what is Clemontis Regis?" Uncle Pinky asked, almost as if he feared the answer.

"A Dalmatian. Back-and-white spotted. A real beauty of a show dog. I don't think I'll breed Dalmatians though. I'd rather have something really far out. A pair of Basenji. They're the dogs that can't bark, you know."

"They ought to make them all that way," Uncle Pinky wisecracked.

The audience went into fits of laughter. Quacky didn't think Uncle Pinky had said anything that funny. Then he noticed . . . some stagehands were holding up cards telling everyone to laugh.

Anybody could be funny that way, Quacky thought.

"You must be kidding about the dogs," Uncle Pinky told Quacky. "You'll use the thousand dollars for the Charles Q. Carlisle Foundation to research your pet project — finding a way to make termites stop chewing. A check will be made out to the Foundation."

The audience began clapping.

"Oh, but I'd rather have the cash," Quacky insisted.

"Impossible," Uncle Pinky said. "You're a minor. Any prize money you win today will automatically be placed in the Charles Q. Carlisle Foundation. Audience, isn't that wonderful and generous of our young genius here? To devote his life and give his money to making termites harmless? Let's all hear it for Charlie Carlisle!"

The band blared more circus music and the men with cards held them up as the audience began stomping, cheering, and hooting.

Quacky had taken some interest in winning the fun and games. Now he began to lose it. What he wanted was to get out of there.

"Now, for our first bit of fun," announced Uncle Pinky. "And if the lovely ladies onstage will open the left curtain, we will see what surprise is in store for our young genius."

Two pretty girls in tights and spangles pulled at ropes that opened the curtain on the left side of the stage. The audience went crazy, laughing at the sight of a diving board on stage. It nearly reached the ceiling, and a small but deep glass-walled container of water stood beneath it. A pole ran down from the diving board to the container and into the water.

"Our first bit of fun this afternoon," said Uncle Pinky, "will be to watch Charlie Carlisle, boy genius, ascend the steps to the top of the diving board blindfolded. Then he will take hold of the pole at the top and ride it down into the tank below."

"But I can't swim!" Quacky protested. His words, however, did not carry over the cheering and clapping.

Someone came up behind Quacky and blindfolded him. Then Uncle Pinky led him to the base of the scaffold on which the diving board was perched.

"Up you go, you smart little monster," Uncle Pinky said, but the audience didn't hear that either. Lifting him up by the seat of his pants, Uncle Pinky started Quacky climbing up the ladder to the top of the diving board.

Quacky couldn't think of a way out, so he kept climbing.

I'll get that thousand dollars away from those termites, Quacky told himself with every rung of the ladder he climbed.

When he got to the top, he was glad he couldn't look down.

"Take hold of the greased pole," Uncle Pinky shouted up to Quacky. "Just ride it down. It'll make sure you land in the water and not on the floor of the stage."

The audience clapped and whistled and the band began playing another circus march.

"I thought they did this to drum rolls," Quacky muttered, but no one heard him.

To back down now and not jump into the tank was unthinkable, Quacky decided. He was up there, he'd get down and win that prize money. And he would buy himself a couple of Basenji dogs to breed. He would become a millionaire so Aunt Maggie wouldn't have to shoplift anymore. And he could live with her and stay out of any other orphanages. All he had to do was jump into the water. Somehow he would get the thousand dollars away from the Charles Q. Carlisle Foundation and those stupid termites.

The music stopped. The audience fell silent. As Quacky expected, the drum rolls began. He knew what he was expected to do when they stopped. He was going to have to jump into the tank.

Keep rolling, you drums, he prayed. Don't stop now! I haven't gotten up my courage yet to jump!

The drums rolled on and on. At last they stopped. It was so quiet, you could hear a pin drop, but none did.

The audience and Uncle Pinky and all his helpers stood with their mouths open. They were waiting for Charlie Carlisle, boy genius, to take a flying leap into the water tank. Even if he was only supposed to ride the pole down.

"Jump!" Uncle Pinky ordered, safely down below.

"*You* jump!" Quacky shouted from above.

In the silence that filled the studio, everyone heard him. It was so unexpected, the audience began laughing. Quacky couldn't see with his blindfold on, but he was sure none of the stagehands were holding up laugh cards.

Quacky knew there was still only one honorable way down for him. He closed his eyes, even though he couldn't see under the blindfold. He saw himself living at Aunt Maggie's house in Smedley, Connecticut, with hundreds of pedigree dogs. He took a deep breath, took hold of the greased pole, and jumped.

In the instant he leaped off the diving board, an unexpected commotion broke out below, which Quacky heard only vaguely.

"That boy up there is an imposter!" someone shouted. Quacky was on his way down now. "He's not Charles Q. Carlisle. *Here* is the real Charles Q. Carlisle, boy genius!"

Uncle Pinky and the studio audience and thousands of viewers all over the country watched as the real Charlie Carlisle was pushed into the studio by his parents and agent. He was a skinny, pale little boy, neatly dressed in a green suit with a bow tie and large glasses.

"Arrest that boy!" someone shouted, pointing to Quacky. This, Quacky heard clearly, just as he hit the water.

Stagehands helped Quacky out of the water tank. In the confusion, dripping wet, Quacky slipped out of their hands. He ran into the real Charles Q. Carlisle, accidentally knocking him down and getting him all wet.

"You and your termites!" Quacky told him, not stopping to help him up.

He ran for the curtains and for the next few minutes gave Uncle Pinky, the stagehands, and Charlie Carlisle's parents and agent a merry chase. He went in and out the curtains onstage and past the other fun and games set up for the show.

He passed a lion's cage with a real lion inside, roaring. There was a slide that ran down from the ceiling to the floor where a bucket of mud waited to catch the slider. And there was something that, to Quacky, looked like a torture chamber, with spikes sticking out of the sides. But he couldn't be sure, because he was moving so fast.

Somehow, in all the chasing, Quacky scooped up his old clothes. Then he saw a door.

He opened it and shut it quickly behind him. He found himself in a large dark room that was so quiet he couldn't hear a sound.

Off in the distance, he saw a faint light. As he started for it, he noticed that it was a street lamp. An odd thing, he thought . . . a street lamp inside a building.

Suddenly he saw a man standing under the street lamp, lighting a cigarette. Then, from behind the man, with his back to Quacky, another man appeared. He was holding a knife whose blade flashed in the glow of the lamp.

"Watch out!" Quacky warned the man lighting his cigarette. "That man behind you has a knife!"

The man with the knife turned, and, open-mouthed, looked at Quacky.

"What the blazes are you doing on the set?" the man with the knife demanded, astonished.

"Get that kid out of here!" someone called out from the darkness behind Quacky.

"Who *is* that?" someone else asked.

The lights went on and Quacky realized his mistake. It was another television studio!

"We'll have to reshoot the scene!" a voice cried. "Thank heaven we're on film and not live! Get that kid *out* of here!"

Stagehands from *Killer-Diller*, the weekly murder mystery, began chasing Quacky. He looked frantically for another door.

Still wet from his dunking, clutching his own clothes, Quacky found another door. It led him into another studio, this one brightly lighted, so he could see where he was going. But with the stagehands after him, he was running too fast to avoid knocking over some bowls and pots and pans and plates and food that stood on a long table.

A lady in a white apron, holding a wooden mixing spoon and a bowl, dropped both as she saw her chef's show crashing down all around her.

Quacky, still pursued by stagehands, found another door to enter. This one was the network's newsroom, broadcasting live. Luckily, he entered slowly and quietly, and did not interrupt anyone or knock anyone down or anything over. Except a stack of cardboard signs that had been standing against a wall.

Quacky carefully scooped them up, not certain if they had to be in any proper order. But he managed to get them all back against the wall again without anyone noticing.

He tiptoed his way toward a far door, which he hoped would be the last one he would have to go through to get out of TV Land. Just as he got out the door, he heard someone on the news program announce the weather forecast:

"Ice and sleet, followed by an expected fourteen inches of snow. . . ?"

The weatherman looked puzzled as he read the cardboard sign in front of him.

"Odd weather for July," Quacky noted, going through another door.

PEACE, BUT NOT QUITE QUIET

With so many people after him, running this way and that but mostly in circles, Quacky had little difficulty in getting away from them.

He found a broom closet where he changed out of his wet suit and into his old clothes. When he peeked his head out the door he saw some people in line by an elevator. A young man in a uniform was talking to them, and Quacky could see he was a guide, taking them on a tour of the building. Quacky left the broom closet and fell in with the tour, riding down the elevator with it to the ground floor. Soon he was outside again.

The sun was nice and warm and Quacky

was glad it wasn't going to snow fourteen inches.

Weather forecasters don't really know what the weather's going to be the next day anyway, Quacky thought. Unless they wait until morning and look out the window.

Quacky wanted to get home again. Back to Smedley, Connecticut, and find Aunt Maggie. He hoped she was not in jail again.

It was only an hour and a half by train from New York to Smedley and nearly twice that by bus. It didn't matter much to Quacky, because he didn't have fare for either.

He asked someone where the nearest bus station was, and walked twelve blocks to get to it. The sun helped him to dry off and he felt good again, wearing his own clothes.

At the bus depot he learned that a bus was leaving in a few minutes for Connecticut, and making a stop at Smedley. But the fare, even if it had been only a dime, was more than he could afford.

He would have to sneak a ride, Quacky decided, but how? A long line of people were waiting to hand their tickets and luggage to the driver of a bus under a sign that said "Connecticut." Most of the bus was already full of passengers, and Quacky was worried that the last seat might be taken before he could think of a way to get aboard.

But then he had an idea. He got in line behind a lady carrying a large suitcase. When she set it down to move up a few inches in the line, he quickly tested one of the latches and found it could be opened, so he opened it. Then he waited in line a little longer.

As more passengers got on the bus, the line got shorter and the lady moved her suitcase up another few inches. Soon she was next in line to hand the driver her ticket. As she held it out to the man, Quacky undid the second latch on her suitcase.

The driver punched her ticket and took up her suitcase. As he lifted it off the ground, the suitcase flew open and all its contents, including the lady's underwear, spilled out at their feet.

In the confusion, as the driver helped the lady scoop her things back into her suitcase, Quacky sneaked aboard the bus. He went immediately to the toilet in the back of the bus and locked himself in. He didn't come out until he felt the bus moving.

He might not have found a vacant seat, but his luck held. There was one empty seat in the back of the bus by the window, and Quacky wondered why no one had taken it. It seemed to be one of the most desirable seats on the whole bus.

Halfway to Smedley, when the bus stopped for a coffee break at a restaurant and he got off to stretch, Quacky realized why no one had taken his seat. He couldn't straighten up! He had to walk doubled over, and he could hardly breathe.

"Your seat's over one of the rear wheels," one of the passengers explained. "The jarring can throw out your back."

"I can't make up my mind," Quacky replied slowly, "whether to die here on the highway halfway between New York and Smedley, Connecticut, or go on and die in Smedley. I guess I'd rather die in familiar surroundings, so I'll go on."

When the bus got rolling again, rather than go back to the seat over the rear wheel, Quacky made himself comfortable on the seat in the toilet. He relinquished it from time to time as it was needed more urgently by others.

When the bus driver called out "Smedley," Quacky could hardly move. Another passenger had to help him off and he found it impossible to straighten up. He was glad no one was after him, because he wasn't sure he could walk, let alone run.

Quacky walked slowly out of the bus station, so doubled up that he couldn't lift his head. When he reached the curb, he stepped down and walked to the center stripe in the road and dropped to his knees, falling into a pile like a department-store dummy.

Two cars coming from opposite directions screeched to a stop just before running him over, and a policeman blew his whistle to hold up traffic while he investigated.

Both motorists, a lady and an old man, insisted they had not come even close to running down the boy.

"Someone must have hit me," Quacky told the policeman, "because I didn't come into the world this way."

"We'd better call an ambulance," the policeman said, "and figure out later which one of you hit him."

While both motorists kept swearing they were innocent, an ambulance arrived. Quacky was strapped to a stretcher and taken to Smedley Community Hospital. As the ambulance took him away, a pretty nurse held his hand and told him what a brave boy he was.

He was glad for two reasons that he was

going to the hospital. Someone would fix up his back, and also the hospital was only four blocks from Aunt Maggie's house.

The emergency room must be having a slow day, Quacky judged, from all the fuss and attention he was getting. It was only seconds before a doctor examined him.

"Why, you haven't been hit by a car," the doctor said. "How did you get your back in this condition?"

Quacky told about the bus ride and the doctor had him stretch out on his stomach on an examining table. After a twist of the neck here and a twist of the back there, the doctor told Quacky to get up.

Quacky was surprised to find he not only could stand straight again, but he felt better than he had in a long time.

"How'd you do that?" Quacky asked. He was amazed that after so short a time, he could feel so good again.

"Now I'll tell you what," said the doctor. "Don't tell anyone I practiced chiropractic on you, and I won't charge you. The county doesn't approve of chiropractic. But I say, if a twist here and a twist there will fix a person up, why not?"

"I'll keep your secret, doc, if you'll fix it

with the cop," Quacky bargained. "You're right. I didn't get hit by a car. I just needed a ride to the hospital. My aunt lives near here."

"You're a very resourceful boy," the doctor remarked, pleased with Quacky.

"I don't know when I was born, but my Aunt Maggie says I must be an Aries, because I get into scrapes but always land on my feet. Like a cat with nine lives."

"So your aunt is into astrology," the doctor said.

"She's into astrology like a baseball into a mitt," Quacky admitted, still trying out his arms and legs. "She's a Leo — the lion, you know. And she really is like the Queen of the Jungle!"

"I'd like to talk to you more about astrology," the doctor replied, "but I've got to get back to work. Just keep landing on your feet, son. You'll be all right."

They shook hands and Quacky started on his way home again. He walked straight and tall and felt very good as he saw the sun begin to set behind some pine trees near Aunt Maggie's house.

But he was disappointed when he didn't see any lights on in the house. He was sure now that Aunt Maggie wasn't home. She must be in jail again.

He went to the mailbox on the front porch. She often left Quacky notes and the house key in the mailbox when she was gone and expected him to turn up.

The box was nearly full of mail, Quacky thought. That's good. It means Aunt Maggie must have been gone awhile and should be ready to come home.

He found a collection of bills, some advertising mail, a sample of some toothpaste, and a letter addressed to him. He could feel a key inside the envelope before he opened it.

"Dear Quacky," the letter began. "I ran short on my Social Security the second of the month and got caught in the supermarket with a small ham and a six-pack of beer. I should be home in a few days. Here's the key. Make yourself comfortable, but don't let in any strangers. Unless they pay you rent. There isn't much to eat in the icebox, but I know you won't starve. You're always able to manage for yourself. See you soon. Much love, Aunt Maggie. P.S. No dogs in the house, please. They're messy devils and I don't want to find anything in the corners. P.P.S. The rest of the month should be a good one for me. My chart says I'm going to find some money!"

Quacky laughed as he folded the letter, put it with the rest of the mail, took the key, and went into the house.

"I sure hope her astrology chart is right," he said to himself.

There wasn't a sound in the house except the ticking of an old school clock on the kitchen wall. Aunt Maggie must have wound it for a week before she left.

He went first to the refrigerator and chuckled at how Aunt Maggie still called it an "icebox." He never knew how old she was, but she must be pretty old. She called everything by its old name.

He found enough milk to fill a glass, and a few slices of lunch meat, but no bread anywhere. Aunt Maggie always made cookies, he knew. He found half a jarful in a cabinet over the sink. They were chewy chocolate-chip cookies. He liked crunchy ones better, but Aunt Maggie was not a very good cookie maker.

He put everything on a footstool in front of the television set. Aunt Maggie had the smallest, oldest black-and-white television set he had ever seen anywhere. It was so old, it had a round screen. The set needed fixing, so everyone looked extra tall and skinny. He didn't mind. He seldom watched the tube.

But he watched now. It was just six o'clock and he wanted to catch the evening news, hoping NCB might mention him. He turned the set on and sat Indian-style in a high-back stuffed chair as the news came on.

"Everyone in the small town of Smedley, Connecticut, is talking about the biggest news that's happened there since the Civil War, when a Confederate officer rode his horse up the steps of City Hall and took over the town," a newsman was saying.

"Oh, good!" Quacky said. "They're talking about me!"

But he wondered: how did they know he was from Smedley? He didn't remember telling anyone at the television station where he was from. He watched and listened more closely.

"The First National Bank of Smedley was robbed today by a pair of gunmen wearing stocking masks," the newsman went on.

"Oh, they're not talking about me after all." Quacky was disappointed. He was hoping he might have become famous.

"The gunmen got away with a hundred

thousand dollars," the newsman reported. "And a rare collection of some sort that bank officials so far have not identified. It is believed the collection may be of priceless diamonds. Separate rewards are offered for the return of the money and the collection. A thousand dollars is offered for each."

Quacky whistled long and low. What he couldn't do with a thousand dollars or two!

"Now to local news. . . . Several of our station's afternoon programs were interrupted today by a boy posing as Charles Q. Carlisle, the boy genius . . ."

"That's better!" Quacky shouted. "They're finally talking about me!"

"The boy brazenly impersonated Charles Q. Carlisle on *Mid-Day Fun and Games*, going so far as to dive off a high platform into a tank of water. Just as he dived, the real Charles Q. Carlisle arrived in the studio. Studio personnel pursued the boy imposter through several other studios where programs were either on the air live or being taped. The station wishes to take this opportunity to apologize to its viewers. Stricter security precautions will be in force in the future, to keep out undesirable persons."

Undesirable! Quacky slunk back deeply in

his chair and sulked. What an awful thing to say! Especially to an Aries. He liked to be liked! At least Aunt Maggie liked him. That much he knew!

". . . And as a last reminder before signing off tonight's news," the man on the television screen went on, "we repeat tomorrow's weather forecast. 'Ice and sleet followed by fourteen inches of snow' was an erroneous report given earlier today by accident. Sunny skies and a high tomorrow of eighty are expected. Please ignore the earlier forecast."

They didn't show pictures of me running around in their studios, Quacky thought, disappointed. But at least the announcer didn't say anyone is after me. Maybe they'll just forget about me. I hope so.

As he turned off the television, Quacky heard someone knocking at the back door. He got up and went into the kitchen. The shade was drawn and he couldn't see who was outside. Maybe Aunt Maggie had come home.

"Who's there?" he asked.

"Gas man, to read the meter," a man's voice replied from outside.

"Wait a minute," Quacky said. "I'll unlock the door."

He took the house key out of his pocket,

31

opened the door, and looked into the muzzies of two guns being held on him. Two men wearing stocking masks pushed their way past him into the kitchen and locked the door behind them.

Quacky put two and two together fast, and wondered what he was going to be in for.

LONESOME NO MORE

"You do what you're told, sonny, and we won't blow your head off!" one of the masked gunmen said. He was big and tall and looked like a wrestler. He wore an expensive-looking cream-colored suit with a blue shirt and a tie covered with printed flowers.

"Don't frighten the boy," the other gunman told him, taking off his mask. He was not built as large as the other man, and was younger. He looked like some of the lumberjacks or rodeo riders Quacky had seen in the movies. His face was deeply tanned and Quacky liked his looks. He was impressed with the shiny striped shirt and white knit slacks the man wore.

"You two sure are sharp dressers," Quacky said quickly. "Want some cold beer? My Aunt Maggie has a couple of cans left in the refrigerator. She's in jail, so you might as well drink them."

"Get this kid!" Shiny Shirt told Flower Tie. "We bust into his house with masks and guns and he compliments us on our duds and offers us beer. Get the beer, kid, and we'll talk."

Quacky got the two cans of beer and asked if they wanted glasses.

"Cans is good enough," Shiny Shirt said, eagerly taking one and popping the ring on the lid. He swallowed deeply and wiped his mouth off, smiling.

"Is it really okay to take off our masks?" Flower Tie asked.

"How can you drink beer with your mask on?" Quacky inquired.

"None of your lip, kid," Flower Tie said. He decided it would be all right after all to take off his stocking mask, since his companion already had.

"We're gonna stay here awhile," Shiny Shirt told Quacky. "Until the heat cools off."

"It isn't supposed to get higher than eighty tomorrow," Quacky said. "I'm sorry we don't have air conditioning."

"The kid's a real gas." Shiny Shirt laughed. "No, I mean that while the cops are after us, we'd like to stay here. Listen to me! 'Like to stay here!' As if we couldn't, if we wanted to! And we want to!"

"My Aunt Maggie left me a note in the mailbox, saying not to let any strangers in. Unless they pay rent."

Flower Tie grunted, but Shiny Shirt laughed again.

"Get a load of this kid," Flower Tie said, drinking his beer. "We should pay him rent! Kid, didn't I tell you we could blow your head off?"

"And didn't I tell you not to scare the boy?" Shiny Shirt asked his partner. "What's this about your aunt being in jail? What's she in for? There ain't gonna be no cops snooping around here because of her, are there?"

"I doubt it," Quacky replied. "She just shoplifted a small ham and a six-pack of beer from the supermarket. She doesn't get much from Social Security. So she picks extra things up now and then. They usually let her come home after a day or two. And when she does, no one ever comes with her."

"They'd better not," Shiny Shirt said.

"Let's talk about it over a pizza. I'm starved. You have a phone in the house?"

"If Aunt Maggie paid her phone bill last month." Quacky went to the phone on a small table next to the television set in the living room and said it worked.

"Then call the best pizza place in town," Shiny Shirt ordered. "And get us three large. What you want on yours, Clem?"

It was the first time Quacky had heard either of them call the other by his name. So Flower Tie was Clem.

"Hey, what's this telling-my-name business?" Clem demanded.

"Hey, kid," Shiny Shirt said to Quacky. "My name is Jerry and this here is Clem. They're not our real names. Just names you can call us."

"Pepperoni and mushrooms," Clem told Quacky.

"Sausage and anchovies for me," Jerry said.

"I'm a sausage-and-anchovies man myself," said Quacky.

"Then order three large and ask them to send two six-packs of beer and some Cokes for you," Jerry said. "Make sure they're cold!

Will they get suspicious, sending an order like that to this house?"

"Aunt Maggie sometimes orders half a dozen pizzas, for her bridge club," Quacky said. "I'll just say it's for the club."

"Smart kid," Jerry remarked to Clem.

Quacky ordered the pizzas and drinks without any problems. Then he showed the bank robbers around the house.

"Some nice old furniture," Jerry observed. "Your aunt must be rich. Or someone died and left her some heirlooms."

Quacky laughed. "Aunt Maggie rich? She's about the poorest person in Smedley! But she likes good things and finds them at house sales and garage sales. It's amazing what some people toss out or sell for practically nothing."

"Well, for an old house, the place has some neat stuff," Clem agreed.

"Do you have the hundred thousand dollars with you?" Quacky asked Jerry. "And the collection? What *is* the collection?"

"Sure, we got the money and stuff with us," Jerry admitted. "You don't think we'd take a chance leaving it somewhere."

"I just wondered what a hundred thousand dollars looks like," Quacky said.

"Show him," Jerry told Clem.

Clem emptied his pockets on the table in the dining room. He spread out stacks of crisp, new paper money that made Quacky's eyes nearly pop out.

"And what about the collection?" Quacky asked.

"That's outside," Jerry said. "In your milk box. Bring it in, okay? And don't try running away, because remember, we're armed."

"I won't run away." Quacky went to the back door and Clem and Jerry watched as he recovered a metal box from inside the wooden box where Aunt Maggie had milk delivered just outside the back door.

"Bring it here," Jerry called from the dining room.

Quacky brought the metal box to Jerry and watched as the lid was opened. He suddenly realized that neither Jerry nor Clem knew what was inside!

"Well I'll be. . . ." Jerry was amazed at what he saw.

"Toy soldiers!" Quacky exclaimed.

"But look at them!" Clem said. "They look like they can march and do things."

Jerry picked one out of the box. It was a drummer boy. He wound it and they all laughed as it began to beat the drum and walk across the table.

"Hey, look at this!" Jerry was studying the inside of the box, which held a couple dozen mechanical toy soldiers. "There's an engraving. It says: 'From the private collection of Chester MacDougall.'"

"That's the president of the Smedley Bank!" Quacky informed them. "I heard his name on TV. The newsman said no one would identify the collection that was stolen, not even the bank president, Chester MacDougall."

Jerry laughed. "So the bank president collects toy soldiers! No wonder he didn't want to tell what the collection was! He don't want everybody to know he plays with kids' toys!"

"He's got a thousand-dollar reward out for the collection," Quacky said. "And another thousand for return of the money."

"Maybe we can think of a way to get that thousand-dollar reward for the soldiers." Jerry looked at Clem. "We wouldn't want to embarrass the bank president. Maybe we could add another grand to our loot, before we leave town."

Jerry and Clem took the other toy soldiers out of the metal box. They wound them up and watched as the small army paraded across the dining-room table. One soldier tooted a trumpet that made noise. Another banged cymbals together.

"I'll bet these are worth more than a grand," Quacky said.

"I'll bet you're right," Jerry agreed. "But I'll bet that bank president would do just about anything to keep his collection a secret."

"We'd better put them back in the box," Clem suggested, "before we break any of them."

Jerry nodded. "They're worth a lot more working than busted. You, now, kid. You be sure not to go playing with these soldiers when we're not looking. But no chance of that, because one of us is gonna be watching you every minute. So you don't run away."

"I wouldn't run away," Quacky assured them. "I just got back from half a dozen orphanages and foster homes. I just want to stay with Aunt Maggie. But she keeps shoplifting and getting sent to jail. She should be back home any day now."

"We'll be going in a day or two, won't we?" Clem asked Jerry.

"Maybe," Jerry replied. "We'll see. Depends on how hard they go looking for us. And how comfortable and safe our young friend here can make us. What's *your* name, by the way?"

Quacky gave them his full name. Then the name he preferred for short. They said the short version was okay with them.

The doorbell rang.

"See if it's the pizza man," Jerry warned Quacky. "Here are two ten-dollar bills. They ought to more than cover it. We'll be watching, behind the dining room drapes. If you let on to us, or make a wrong move, you're gonna regret it."

"I won't make any mistakes," Quacky promised. "I don't want my head blown off. Besides, I haven't had a good pizza in months."

Jerry and Clem hid behind the dining room drapes with their guns drawn and watched as Quacky checked on who was outside.

"It's okay," Quacky told them from the window next to the door. "It's the pizza man."

Quacky got the pizzas and drinks and paid the delivery man. He tipped him fifty cents.

"I thought he'd get suspicious if I tipped him more," Quacky said. "And if I didn't tip him enough, he might not come back."

"What do we want him coming back for?" Clem asked. "You give him some kind of signal about us?"

"No, I didn't," Quacky said. "I just thought you might be staying around and want to order other things from time to time. They have fried chicken and barbecued spare ribs and french-fried shrimp and . . ."

"Stop it already!" Clem cried. "I want an order of each, I'm so hungry!"

"Eat your pizza!" Jerry told him.

They all got into comfortable chairs in the living room with their pizzas. Quacky turned on the television set while they opened their beers and Coke.

"Hey, maybe there's a good bank robbery movie on!" Clem said.

"I've had enough bank robberies for one day," Jerry replied, tearing into his pizza. After he took his first bite, he smiled contentedly. "Quacky, you sure know where to order pizza. This is the best I've had in years."

Quacky tore into his and agreed. "You know," he said, "you two don't act much like bank robbers and gunmen. At least, not like the ones I've seen on TV."

"We don't rob banks for a living," Jerry replied. "Times got tough for us. We had to do something. We needed a job. Clem's a terrific carpenter and was teaching me the trade when we both got laid off, six months ago.

Our unemployment money didn't last long. You ever drift for six months without knowing where your next pizza was coming from? Or where you'd lay your head at night?"

Quacky told them about the places he'd lived. And how everyone was always keeping him from living with his Aunt Maggie.

"She only takes things because she doesn't have enough to live on," Quacky said. "She likes nice things, and can't afford them. She's a Leo, you see."

"She's a what?" Clem asked.

"A Leo," Quacky repeated. "You know . . . the zodiac sign. Her birthday is August twentieth. Leos like nice things, and it's rough when they can't afford them. That's why she buys things from house sales."

"Maybe if she can't afford things, she shouldn't take them," Clem suggested. "Like from the supermarket."

"Look who's talking!" Jerry retorted.

"Your Aunt Maggie ain't a weirdo, is she?" Clem asked Quacky. "Is she spooky, about this astrology stuff?"

"Spooky? I don't think so. She just knows a lot about it. She'll tell you all about yourself, if you tell her when you were born."

"No thanks," Clem said. "I can do without that. With luck, I won't ever have the pleasure of meeting your Aunt Maggie."

"Anyway, Quacky," said Jerry, "I just want you to know, we never did any harm to anyone before. We just needed a little money. Heck, we wish that bank teller hadn't given us so much. I told him, 'Hand over five hundred bucks.' But he dug under the counter and came up with a sackful of money! Then as if that wasn't enough, he pushed that stupid box into my hand. Now every cop in the state is after us, and probably the F.B.I. too!"

"We just wanted five hundred fish," Clem said. "To tide us over until we could get a job."

"Can't you give all the money back, except for a couple hundred dollars?" Quacky asked. "You could give the soldiers back too."

"Well," Clem replied, "we already got all the money, and the soldier collection too. It would be a shame to give them up."

They went back to watching television. Quacky flicked the dial and stopped.

"Hey, look!" he said. "Tonight's mystery movie is about to come on. And it's called *The Big Bank Heist*!"

"What else's on?" Jerry asked.

HOUSE GUESTS

They watched a comedy instead. Afterward, Jerry and Clem took turns taking showers upstairs in Aunt Maggie's bathroom.

"I never saw so many women's things!" Clem complained to Jerry. "I never knew a woman could *wear* so many things! No wonder it takes them so long to get dressed!"

It was a warm night, no women were around, and they had nothing else to wear to bed, so Jerry and Clem just wore their shorts.

"Does one of us have to stay awake and watch the kid while the other sleeps?" Clem asked Jerry.

"I've a better idea," Jerry said. He took

Quacky by an arm. "Your Aunt Maggie got a bed in the house that's big enough for the three of us? You in the middle, so we'll know if you walk in your sleep."

"No bed that big," Quacky replied. "Just her bed and one in the room I sleep in, or used to."

"Then we've got to put the two mattresses together on the floor somewhere, for the three of us," Jerry said.

It made a big enough bed for them, but Quacky was not too happy in the middle, where the two mattresses met. Even a blanket folded over the ridges did not smooth them down.

The discomfort of the bed was made up for in the companionship, Quacky decided. He felt good about being close to two men old enough to be his father. Even if they were bank robbers. And he was beginning to like Jerry. Clem he wasn't sure about.

When the lights were turned off in Quacky's bedroom and all three were as comfortable as they could expect to be, Quacky said good night to them. With his eyes closed, Quacky's imagination went to work. He knew why: he was an Aries and they were always dreaming up things.

Before he knew it, he was seeing himself

in the sky. He was riding a white horse with wings, and Jerry was a sultan or someone, riding the same horse and holding Quacky in front of him. They were flying over some castle and someone was high in a window, telling them they had to come down. When they flew closer, he saw it was the lady with a nose like a pickle.

He worked his imagination as hard as he could and got them to fly over the castle and off away from the pickle lady. Quacky sighed and fell asleep.

Sunlight streaking through the curtains awakened Quacky first. He looked quickly to see if Jerry was still there. He was, and Quacky was relieved. Clem was there too, but Quacky didn't care as much about that.

He hoped his house guests would stay a long time, whether they paid rent or not. At least he hoped Jerry would. He knew they would buy his meals. That would be plenty in exchange for staying at the house.

He began to worry about them. They were, after all, bank robbers. But he believed Jerry when he said they only meant to rob the bank of five hundred dollars.

They're just out-of-work carpenters, Quacky decided. Even if they did use guns. Not bank robbers. No more than Aunt Maggie was a crook.

Somewhere in the back of his head something told Quacky as he lay awake: "Stealing's stealing, Quacky. A rose is a rose is a rose. Call a spade a spade. You steal something and you're a crook. No two ways about it."

Quacky would listen no more to his conscience. He decided to get up and make coffee for his house guests.

As he started up from the mattress, he felt a hand grasp his right ankle and pull him down.

"And where do you think you're going?" Jerry demanded, yawning.

"Thought I'd make you men some coffee."

"Tell you what." Jerry turned over onto his back, the sheet covering him from the chest down. "You go downstairs and make us some coffee. But you whistle or sing or talk or keep making some kind of noise, so I know you're down there and not on the telephone or running outside. If I hear you stop making some kind of noise, even for two seconds, I'll be down there with my gun. Don't forget . . . we're only part-time bank robbers. But we *are* bank robbers!"

Jerry was not quite awake and he looked funny. His sandy-colored hair was all mussed

48

from sleeping, his eyes were puffy, and he needed a shave. Otherwise, Jerry was a good-looking man. Clem, Quacky could see, looked like a bum.

"I'll start with whistling." Quacky smiled at Jerry. "Don't worry. I won't run off. This is my home."

"What about that rent you talked about last night?" Jerry asked.

"Aunt Maggie *did* say to charge strangers rent. It would help her out a little too. When she gets back from jail."

"Do me a favor?" Clem yawned himself awake. "Don't say that word around me anymore? Gives me the willies."

"Sure," Quacky said. "I understand. Let's consider Aunt Maggie on vacation, not in the you-know-where."

"How much rent do you want from us?" Jerry asked. "Careful now — remember you're dealing with bank robbers."

"By the day or week?" Quacky asked.

"Better charge us by the day," Jerry said. "But you know, I kind of hope we stay here awhile. I'm getting to like it."

"How about five dollars a day," Quacky suggested.

"Sounds fair," said Jerry.

"Apiece?" Quacky asked.

"You drive a hard bargain, but okay," Jerry said. "My pants are over the chair in the corner. The white ones, remember? Take ten bucks out of the right pocket. But don't cheat. Anything I hate, it's a cheater and a thief."

Quacky gave Jerry a sly look. He took two five-dollar bills out of Jerry's pocket and showed them. Then he went downstairs with his clothes and dressed in the kitchen, whistling "Old MacDonald Had a Farm." He made up words of his own to sing: "Old MacDougall had some toys . . ."

"You know, that's some kid," Jerry said to Clem as they were getting up. "I'd never leave a kid like that. Like his father did. Not if I could help it."

"Maybe his father couldn't help it," Clem said. "Lots of things in this life we can't help."

"We can help most of it," Jerry said.

Jerry showered and shaved. He put on his white pants and shiny striped shirt and went downstairs while Clem went back to sleep.

"Coffee's almost ready," Quacky told him. "I sure think you're a swell dresser, Jerry."

"I wish I had more clothes," Jerry said. "I'm nuts about nice clothes. This stuff I'm wearing is the last of what once was a pretty neat wardrobe. Had to sell it all, little by little. I guess my liking for clothes comes from when

I was a kid, even younger than you. All I got to wear was hand-me-downs, from my brothers and uncles. And *those* were tough times, I want you to know. I remember walking about a dozen blocks to school one morning in a blizzard, wearing my sister's gym shoes. My shoes were in the shoemaker's and I didn't have anything else to wear. My feet felt cold for a week after!"

Quacky poured a cup of coffee and handed it to Jerry. "Sorry there's no cream or sugar."

"Black's fine. Matches my mood."

"They won't catch you," Quacky reassured Jerry. "Not if I can help it!"

"You stay out of it," Jerry ordered. "I don't want you becoming an accomplice before or after the fact. If we get caught, you tell the cops we held you at gunpoint. We made you let us stay here. Just don't mention about the rent."

"Do you have a wife and kids, back home?" Quacky asked. He'd been trying to get up nerve enough to ask and finally had.

"Me?" Jerry asked. "No way! I'm not the family type. Just want to make a living and drink some beer, bowl when I want to bowl, take long walks when I want to, and find . . . companionship when I want. I'm a loner, I guess."

Quacky knew all about loners, and how lonely they could be. Most of the time he was a loner too.

"What's your birth sign?" Quacky asked.

"You mean that zodiac stuff?" Jerry asked over his coffee. "I'm a Gemini. But I warn you . . . I don't dig astrology. I guess I'm just not a 'believer.' "

"A Gemini," Quacky repeated. "I've picked up some stuff from Aunt Maggie. She's the expert. That's swell, you being a Gemini."

"What's swell about it?"

"Well, it sort of figures. Aunt Maggie can tell you lots more about yourself, but from what little I know, you're okay. You're a drifter, though. You come and go like the wind."

"That's me, all right. What else?"

"You don't like being tied down." Quacky could tell Jerry was the type to come and go, and he was already afraid he would be going soon.

"How do I turn out?" Jerry asked.

"Predicting the future is for gypsy fortune-tellers," Quacky chuckled. "Astrology just tells you what you're like."

"If you say so. How about some more hot?" Jerry held out his cup and Quacky filled it again.

One of the first things he would do when Aunt Maggie came home would be to ask her all about Gemini people. Something inside Quacky told him that Jerry was a good guy.

"How about Clem?" Quacky asked.

"I don't know when he was born!" Jerry almost laughed. "I hardly know his name!"

"I mean, does he have a wife and kids?"

"No, but he probably will, someday. I don't know about me, though. You're right . . . I don't like being tied down."

Their conversation was interrupted by a voice at the back door.

"Quacky?" someone called. "You back home?"

"Who's that?" Jerry asked. He took his gun from the front of his belt and aimed it at the door.

"Sounds like my pal, Ralph," Quacky said. "He must have seen our lights on last night. You can put your gun away. He won't be any trouble."

"You'd just better get rid of him. And don't tell him about Clem and me!"

"He'll become suspicious if I don't talk to him," Quacky said. "And he's probably got Clemontis Regis with him."

"Who's that?"

"His pedigree Dalmatian."

"Now we're being tracked by bloodhounds!" Jerry held the gun more firmly. "You can let Ralph in, but not his dog. I'll be right in the next room, so stay in the kitchen with Ralph. And get rid of him fast, you hear?"

"Don't worry," Quacky assured him. "I'll handle it."

After Jerry hid himself in the dining room, Quacky let Ralph in.

"Not Reggie," Quacky told him. "Aunt Maggie's not home yet. But she left a note saying no dogs in the house."

"Reggie isn't just any old dog," Ralph replied proudly. He came into the kitchen but left Clemontis Regis outside. "He's a pedigree blue-ribbon, trophy-winning special dog. I'm going to breed him, and his pups will sell for . . ."

". . . I know, a thousand dollars apiece," Quacky finished. "But he still has to stay outside. Aunt Maggie's afraid a dog might leave things in the corners."

Reggie clawed at the back door and whined but it did him no good.

"Big baby," Quacky said. "You say he won a blue ribbon and a trophy?"

"Best of his class, last week at the County Dog Show," Ralph boasted.

"I'll be the owner of a pair of pedigree show

dogs real soon," Quacky said. "Some real blue-blood Basenji."

"They cost two or three hundred dollars each," Ralph said. "Where are you going to get money like that?"

"I just feel lucky. Like money's going to come my way, and pretty soon. At least, money is in Aunt Maggie's horoscope. And we always share."

"You believe in that astrology bunkum?" It was obvious to Quacky that Ralph didn't.

"Well, sometimes it sure hits the nail on the head," Quacky said.

"Sure, and the moon's full of applesauce," Ralph retorted. "What are you doing home for, anyway? How'd you get away this time?"

"I just left the County Home. They were so busy, having an art fair, they never noticed when I hopped on the back of a panel truck and rode out with the garbage."

"They're going to get tired of looking for you someday and put you somewhere where you can't get out," Ralph said.

"I can get out of anywhere," Quacky bragged. "Did you hear about that boy in New York yesterday, impersonating Charlie Carlisle, the boy genius, and busting up half a dozen TV shows?"

"Yeah, I heard about it. So what?"

"You're looking at him." Quacky threw his shoulders back. "I never had such a wild time! Just trying to get away from stagehands. If they'd have caught me, I would have been sent back to the County Home for sure. But I'm home now, and for good. When Aunt Maggie gets out of jail, I'm gonna stay here with her."

"They won't let you, though," Ralph said. "Not for long. They'll say she's a crook and a bad influence on you. And they'll send you back to the County Home."

"When I get me a pair of Basenji dogs and start breeding them, I'll make enough money from the pups so Aunt Maggie can stop stealing. We'll have more money than we'll know how to spend. Then no one will send me away again," Quacky replied.

"Your Aunt Maggie doesn't like dogs. I've heard her say how dumb and dirty they are."

Ralph always seemed to like to rain on somebody else's parade, Quacky thought.

"She wouldn't mind if we had a pair of pedigree Basenji that could make us rich," he said. "I bet she wouldn't mind a bit what they did in the corners."

Ralph changed the subject. "I came over to get you. Some of the guys are getting a softball game up. How about it?"

"Can't," said Quacky. "Got to get things cleaned up here. Maybe later I'll come by the field, if I can. But I'll be pretty busy here for a few days. I've got to find a way to get some money, to buy those Basenji."

"Well, good luck." Ralph started for the door. "You'll need a lot of that."

After Ralph left the house and took Clemontis Regis with him, Jerry returned to the kitchen. He stuck his gun back into the front of his belt.

"You did okay," he told Quacky. "You really mean it, about breeding show dogs?"

"It's the only way I know to get enough money so Aunt Maggie won't have to steal," Quacky said. "Then the County will let me stay here with her."

"It isn't such a bad idea," Jerry remarked. "Only thing is the initial expense. Buying a pair of Basenji isn't cheap. You figure it'd cost you about four or five hundred dollars?"

"About." Quacky looked at Jerry with a little smile on his face. "I don't suppose you and Clem would loan me the money? For say ten percent interest in the dogs and their pups?"

"You're a pretty good salesman." Jerry laughed. "But any money we'd loan you would be stolen money. You could go to jail for accepting stolen money."

Quacky was disappointed but could tell that Jerry would like to help him if he could.

"Maybe you could get the reward money for turning in the collection of toy soldiers. That would give you a thousand dollars."

Quacky became immediately interested in Jerry's idea, when Clem entered the kitchen.

"So that's it." Clem poured himself a cup of coffee. "You're willing to put us both on the spot. Letting Quacky play hero and get the reward for returning the soldiers."

Clem was frowning deeply and Quacky knew he was against the idea.

"We've got a hundred thousand dollars," Jerry informed Clem. "We don't need the extra thousand reward money for the soldiers. It'd be too risky for us to return them anyway. The kid and his aunt could make good use of that reward money. And he's earned it. He's been good to us. Besides, when we walked into that bank, all we wanted was five hundred dollars. We've got a couple hundred times that much, and you want more! Being greedy like that could get us caught!"

"We won't get caught if we're smart," said Clem. "And it ain't smart to give the toy collection to the kid. If he turns it in for the reward money, it could be traced back to us, if we stay here."

"We're going *now*!" Jerry decided abruptly. He got up from the table and looked at Quacky. "Before you get involved."

Quacky's heart pounded faster. It was so sudden. He'd had a gnawing fear inside him ever since he met Jerry that Jerry would be leaving soon. He didn't think it would be *that* soon.

"You don't have to go on my account," Quacky told them. "I can take care of myself. I always have. I don't need the reward money to get me a pair of show dogs. I'll get the money somehow."

The front doorbell rang.

"This place is turning into Grand Central Station!" Jerry complained. He took out his gun again and aimed it at the front door in the hall off the living room. "Quacky, see who it is. We'll be hiding behind the drapes in the dining room, watching you. Whoever it is, get rid of him!"

Quacky went to the door and looked out the window from behind the curtains.

"It's okay," he called to Jerry and Clem. "Aunt Maggie's back from . . . vacation!"

A FULL HOUSE

"How thrilling!" Aunt Maggie said, upon being introduced to Jerry and Clem. "Bank robbers! I never thought I'd ever come face-to-face with real, live bank robbers! But you can put your guns away. I won't cause you any trouble. A bag of bones like me?"

Looking at her, Jerry and Clem agreed that it was unlikely she could cause them much trouble. She was tall and very thin. Like many old women with gray hair, she tinted it so it looked steel blue. It was done up on top of her head in tight, flat waves. Few people had seen a hairstyle like that in thirty years. As for her age, it was easy to figure she was still counting after seventy.

She was wearing a lot of make-up, especially rouge. The dress she wore was a bright purple and hung on her like some old curtains, nearly down to her ankles. It had no sleeves and made her thin arms look even skinnier. She had an old handbag hanging from her right wrist, and it was open, revealing a crowded array of things.

Most interesting, Jerry thought, were her shoes. They were silver-colored high-heels, like wedding shoes.

"Help me with this?" Aunt Maggie asked Quacky, giving him a large bag of groceries she had carried in with her.

Quacky looked at her, wondering if she had been shoplifting again.

"It isn't stolen." She laughed. "The policemen at the station were kind enough to take up a small collection. I bought a few things on the way home. Two nice officers drove me. Wasn't that nice?"

"They're outside now?" Jerry asked, looking toward the door.

"No," Aunt Maggie assured him. "They drove me to the supermarket. I walked home from there. You mustn't become so worried, young man. You're perfectly safe here. So long as you don't mess up my place, or harm Quacky or me."

"They've been very neat," Quacky told her. "And they haven't done anything to me. They're even paying rent!"

"Now that *is* thoughtful," Aunt Maggie said. "Now *do* put away those guns. They might go off and break something!"

Jerry and Clem saw that Aunt Maggie was not upset that they were bank robbers. She was going about her business as if they were two long-lost relatives who had just dropped in.

"You must have robbed the Smedley Bank." Aunt Maggie led them into the kitchen. She helped Quacky take things out of the grocery bag and set them on the table. There was a six-pack of cold beer, some cheese, rye bread, pickles, hamburger, and small round tins with fancy labels on them. "Oh, these are delicious!" She held up a tin to Jerry. "Imported Italian pickled eggplant. Tastes like pickles. You'll love them! And are they expensive!"

Clem and Jerry wondered why Aunt Maggie was buying some expensive imported delicacy, when she was obviously as poor as a church mouse. She could tell what they were thinking and smiled.

"When you don't have much," she said, "it's most important to have a little fling now and then, on something lovely but trivial."

Jerry understood. The shiny striped shirt he was wearing was pure silk. It had cost him twenty-five dollars when he couldn't afford to buy a can of beer. But it was great for his morale. And he wore it with great pleasure all the months he was broke, before he and Clem robbed the Smedley bank.

"I don't want you getting the wrong idea about us," Jerry told Aunt Maggie in the kitchen. "We're carpenters by trade, ma'am. We've been out of work a long time and got desperate. We only wanted five hundred dollars, but the bank teller got overly generous and gave us a hundred thousand. We don't want your nephew or you to become involved, so we're gonna leave. Right now."

"Now where are you going to go?" Aunt Maggie asked. She was having such trouble opening the tin of eggplant with a can opener that Jerry finished the job for her. "Every policeman in the state must be out looking for you both. Why don't you just stay here? I can make room for you somehow. I'm a very good cook, when we have the money to buy good cuts of meat. Try this eggplant, you'll love it!"

She delicately lifted a bit of the pickled eggplant into her mouth. She chewed it slowly, tilting her head one way and then another, enjoying it thoroughly.

"Oh, it *is* delicious!" she said. "Try some."

Jerry took a bit, but Clem passed it up.

"Tastes like . . ." Jerry was about to say it tasted like pickled cardboard. But he didn't want to hurt Aunt Maggie's feelings. "Mighty good!"

Aunt Maggie offered Jerry another piece but he politely declined.

"You enjoy it," he told her.

Quacky liked the way Jerry handled the situation. He's a good guy, Quacky thought.

"This is about the looniest . . ." Clem fidgeted. "You sure no cop or probation officer is coming here to check on you?" he asked Aunt Maggie.

"Oh, they're much too busy with bigger fish," Aunt Maggie said. "I'm small potatoes, compared with . . ."

She was about to say, compared with Jerry and Clem. But instead she said, "I've never been visited by the police here at home. All our encounters have been either in the supermarket up the street or at the police station. As for a probation officer, I've never met one."

"What about Quacky?" Jerry asked. "Is anyone likely to come snooping around here for him?"

"It usually takes about a month before they find me," Quacky told him. "All the County red tape, you know. The people at the County Home have to fill out all kinds of forms saying I'm missing, then they have to get them okayed. By the time they send someone out looking for me, I almost turn another birthday."

"Well, if we do stay, we won't stay long," Jerry said.

Quacky was immediately relieved. If they would stay a few days, it would give him time to find a way to get them to stay longer.

"I could use the rent money," Aunt Maggie admitted. She was through with the brined eggplant and into a can of beer. "I never used to drink beer, in the good old days. I still prefer a nice imported French wine. But now I'm glad when I can drink a beer. Join me?"

Both Jerry and Clem looked at the clock on the kitchen wall. When they saw it was only 9:30 A.M., they declined.

"Have you gentlemen had breakfast yet?" Aunt Maggie asked.

They said they hadn't, and she said she could make them some eggs, bacon, toast, waffles, and more hot coffee. But they'd have to send Quacky to the store for it all.

"My stomach's empty as a base drum," Clem complained. "Let's at least stay for breakfast."

"I don't like the idea of Quacky leaving the house," Jerry pointed out. "Without one of us to watch him. But it's too risky for either of us to be seen outside."

"We'll both have to leave the house, sooner or later," Aunt Maggie said. "The neighbors would get suspicious otherwise. You'll simply have to trust us not to tell anyone you're hiding out here."

"Then that makes you accomplices, harboring criminals," Jerry said.

"You said yourself you're not bank robbers, you're carpenters," Aunt Maggie said. "I never heard of any law against letting rooms to carpenters."

They settled it over breakfast after Quacky returned from the grocery store and Aunt Maggie served her new boarders. Either Aunt Maggie or Quacky could leave the house separately, while the other remained home, as a hostage. That way, Jerry and Clem knew neither Quacky nor Aunt Maggie would risk going to the police and turning them in for the reward money. And that way, the neighbors would not get suspicious.

It was Quacky's plan and Jerry congratulated him on it.

"It also proves you and your aunt are being

held prisoners against your will," Jerry said. He was looking relieved about the situation. "So there's no way you can be considered willfully harboring criminals."

"Well, that's settled." Aunt Maggie poured hot coffee into their cups and smiled. "I do wish I had remembered, Quacky . . . to have gotten you some nice chocolate eclairs."

"Funny," said Clem, looking more relaxed than he had looked since he first came to the house. "I don't feel like a criminal. I still feel like a carpenter."

"I know how you gentlemen can keep yourselves busy and your mind off your concerns," Aunt Maggie said. "As you can see, this is an old house. And I just haven't had the money to keep up with things when they go bad. The sewer is all blocked up. Sometimes the toilet won't flush, and the kitchen drain is all plugged. The roof needs repair, the back stairs need fixing or replacing, and just before I was taken to jail last week, a city inspector came. He said I have to have my gutters scraped and painted. Do you know that would cost about four hundred dollars?"

Jerry and Clem looked at Aunt Maggie with their mouths open. They knew what she had in mind: they were carpenters, she needed lots of repair jobs around the house. She would want them to do the work, in trade for their staying there.

"Well," Aunt Maggie said. "The city inspector might send a whole truckful of men here to do something about my gutters, if I don't. And men would have to come out to clean out the sewer and fix my pipes in the kitchen and bathroom. And roofers would be climbing all over the roof. And . . ."

"Okay, lady." Clem set down his cup of coffee. "We get the drift."

"Well, maybe a few small jobs," Jerry said. "We *don't* want city inspectors around, or a lot of repairmen either. What needs fixing first?"

"The sewer," Aunt Maggie said. "It's full of stuff. I suspect it's roots again, in the sewer line. It'll have to be cleaned out."

Clem wrinkled up his nose. "A smelly, dirty, wet job. Let's go, Jerry. Let's find another house in this hick town that's in better shape!"

Jerry held Clem by an arm and he sat back down.

"We can take turns with the sewer," Jerry said. "It won't be too bad a job, I hope. And Aunt Maggie is right about one thing: I need something to take my mind off things."

"I can keep my mind off things, watching baseball on TV," Clem said.

"Not while I'm down in some sewer!" Jerry said. "We're a team, remember?"

Clem threw up his hands. "Between us we have a hundred thousand fish, and we're gonna go swimming in some dame's sewer!"

He immediately regretted calling Aunt Maggie a "dame." She looked hurt, and Jerry was quick to make it up to her.

"He meant 'grand dame,' " Jerry told her. "Like in the British plays. A lady of high breeding."

Aunt Maggie smiled nicely at Jerry. "You're very kind. I've been studying you, young man. You're a Gemini, aren't you?"

"Why, yes," Jerry said. "Did Quacky tell you?"

"I didn't get a chance," Quacky told him.

"Oh, you've broken a lot of hearts, with your coming and going," Aunt Maggie told Jerry. "But one day you'll settle down. You have to want to take care of someone very much, then you'll assume the responsibility. You have good manners, that shows. And you must read, to know about 'grand dames' in British plays."

"That's uncanny," Jerry said. "You know so much about me!"

"Money isn't that important to you," she said. "You may even give it back."

"Not my half!" Clem protested. "And if you give back your half, you're loonier than . . ."

Aunt Maggie looked at him with arched eyebrows. She hoped he would not say what she was expecting him to say. Jerry looked at Clem too.

"I think I'll take that can of beer now," Clem said.

Aunt Maggie smiled and got him a can from the refrigerator. Quacky was glad Clem hadn't finished his sentence. Aunt Maggie was a proud old lady. She had had her good years and was taking her hard years as well as she could. He respected and loved her.

"You're very fond of children," Aunt Maggie said to Jerry.

Jerry looked at Quacky and Quacky looked back at him.

"If they're like Quacky," Jerry said.

"Oh, not many are like him," Aunt Maggie observed. "Sometimes he's as bad as a boy can be. And sometimes he's as good."

Quacky was feeling uncomfortable, with two people he liked a lot talking about him while he was with them. He got up suddenly.

"I want to buy a magazine about show dogs," he said.

"Later," Clem told him. "Stay put in the house a while."

Quacky busied himself making more toast while the others went on talking at the breakfast table.

"Maybe we *should* return all but a couple of hundred dollars," Jerry suggested. "We've only spent twenty so far. We could keep a little more and give back the other ninety-nine thousand-plus dollars. I know *I'd* sleep better, if I didn't look in the mirror in the morning and see a hundred-thousand-dollar bank robber staring back at me."

"You'll still be seeing a couple-hundred-dollars bank robber staring back at you," Clem replied. "And you can go to the Federal pen for that too!"

"I'd be willing to take my chances on that, I think," Jerry said. "And if a plan I have jelling in my head about the toy soldiers works, we might find ourselves not bank robbers at all. But we're gonna need Quacky's help on that."

"I really think you ought to keep more than just a few hundred," Aunt Maggie intervened. "It seems a shame to short yourself so. And what is that about some toy soldiers?"

They filled Aunt Maggie in on the toy collection. She laughed. "Why, old Mr. Mac-

Dougall, playing with toy soldiers! I'm sure he wouldn't want *that* to get around town!"

"I'm sure not," Jerry agreed.

Quacky suspected that the toy soldiers were part of a plan Jerry was working up. He wondered what it could be.

Someone called from outside, and Jerry whipped out his gun.

"Sounds like Ralph again," Quacky said. "Guess he still wants me to play ball."

"Go on," Jerry said. "Aunt Maggie will stay here while you're gone. As insurance."

"Don't worry." Quacky started for the door. "You can trust me."

Outside, Quacky told his friend, "I'm really not interested in playing ball today. But I do want to start looking for a pair of Basenji. Let's go to the pet shop and see if they have any."

Aunt Maggie stuck her head out the kitchen door and called to Quacky, "Bring back a newspaper."

"Okay," he said. He guessed that Jerry and Clem wanted to read about the bank robbery.

"Hello, Ralph," she added. "They let me out this morning. Give my best to your mother."

"I will," Ralph said. "Nice to have you back."

Quacky and Ralph and Clemontis Regis walked six blocks to the pet shop.

"No, we don't have any Basenji here," said the store owner. "Seldom hear of anyone around Smedley owning one. Or even asking about them. I've a book on them, though. Costs $2.98 plus tax."

"I already read the library's copy, for free," Quacky told him. "I know all about Basenji."

"Strange dogs," said the shop owner. "They can't even bark. Short-haired, wrinkle-faced little things. They're supposed to go back to ancient Egypt. Some think they were the first breed of dog that ever was. They sure cost a lot. Just for four legs and what all dogs do."

"Do you know where I could buy a pair?" Quacky asked.

"I've a dog owner's magazine here," the man said. "You could check the classified ads people put in, to buy and sell pedigree dogs. But this isn't the public library, you know. You'll have to buy a copy and that'll cost you $1.25."

"I'll wait until I can afford to buy the dogs first," Quacky said. "Thanks anyway."

"Well, I made a lot of money talking to you two," the pet shop owner told them as they were leaving.

"You're welcome," Quacky replied over his shoulder.

On the way home, Quacky bought a newspaper. He folded it over without looking at the front page. He didn't want to draw Ralph's attention to it.

"Bet the paper's full of stuff about the bank robbery yesterday," Ralph said. "Can I take a look?"

"Who cares about bank robberies?" Quacky evaded. "I thought we were going to look for some show dogs for me."

"Maybe we ought to take a look at the city dog pound," Ralph suggested. "It's just up ahead about a block."

"They won't have any show dogs there."

"Well, they have dogs. And they'll show 'em."

"Not funny," Quacky replied. "But let's take a look anyway."

The dog pound was in one of half a dozen buildings in the town dumping and recycling yards. The boys could tell which was the pound by all the yelping and barking coming from the farthest one.

When they entered the dog pound, they saw rows of cages in which dogs of every breed and size and shape were barking and yelping

74

and clawing, trying to get out. Two men in tan uniforms were busy working. They were taking a big dog out of its cage and putting it into another. The new cage was closed on all sides, so the dogs inside couldn't see out or claw at anyone.

"We're taking some to put to sleep," one of the workers explained. "See any dogs you want? You'll be saving its life if you take him home with you. Costs only five dollars and they've had all their shots."

"We didn't come for any stray mutts," Quacky told him. "We're looking for a pair of Basenji show dogs."

The men laughed. "You won't find any show dogs in here," one of them said. "Just mutts. But some are nice mutts, you know. Look around and pick one out while we get these into the cage."

"You're going to put that one to sleep too?" Quacky admired the looks of the big dog the men were having such trouble getting into the cage.

"Him and a dozen more, today," the man holding the dog said. "More tomorrow. We've just got too many and not enough people want them. It costs the city too much to feed and keep them. So we have to put them to sleep."

"You gas them," Quacky said. "I read about it once." He shuddered at the thought of someone gassing him. "Does it hurt? Getting gassed?"

"The dog doesn't feel anything," one of the men said. "It just goes to sleep. For good."

"I wish I could take them all," Quacky said. "To keep them from the gas chamber. But my Aunt Maggie wouldn't let me take even one. Even if I wanted a mutt, which I don't."

Quacky felt sorry for the dogs. They reminded him of himself. They were orphans too, but unwanted. At least Aunt Maggie wanted him, and maybe Jerry did too. These poor mutts didn't have anyone who wanted them. They were lost, lost for good.

He didn't feel lost himself, even though he had been in enough homes for lost children to last him a lifetime. Why did everyone refer to him as being lost?

You were "lost" if you didn't have a mother or father, he decided. Or if you didn't have a home, and someone who cared for you and looked out for you. But he had Aunt Maggie, even though the County wouldn't consider her a fit guardian for him.

Would Jerry make a fit guardian for me, Quacky wondered. No. He was a bank robber!

Fat chance that the County would let him be my guardian. Even if he wanted to be!

"Find any you like?" one of the men asked Quacky as they caged the big dog and went for another.

"I'm not really in the market," Quacky replied.

"I've got a dog already," Ralph said. "A show dog, leashed just outside."

Quacky looked down into the cage where a small, jet-black puppy was asleep, curled up in a little ball. It was just stirring and coming awake. Stooping down to look closer he saw that it had long, floppy ears and one white paw and a little white at its throat.

"What kind of dog is this one?" Quacky asked.

The taller of the two men came over and looked inside the cage.

"He's just a mutt," he said. "Part Labrador retriever and part Who Knows? But I'll bet he'll make a smart dog, and a good hunting dog, if he isn't put to sleep."

The puppy stood up and walked to the side of the cage where Quacky stood. It began poking its white paw outside the cage at Quacky in a playful way.

Quacky took the pup's paw and its tail began to wag. "He's shaking hands!" Quacky said.

"He could be trained to do lots of tricks," the tall man said. "You know, a good hunting dog can be sold for a couple hundred dollars. They can bring as much as a show dog, sometimes. Ever give any thought to that? Instead of raising show dogs, you could raise hunting dogs. Show dogs can be pretty spoiled and hard to live with. Hunting dogs are often smarter and make a lot better pals."

Quacky thought about that. A show dog like a Basenji would be worth more than a hunting dog. He and Aunt Maggie could never get rich unless he sold dogs for a lot of money. Besides, he knew nothing about training a hunting dog. It would be a lot easier with a Basenji. Just sell the pups and not have to worry about training them.

"How about it?" the tall man asked. "You want that cute little guy with the white paw?"

Quacky took another look at the puppy. It was standing on its hind legs, reaching out of the cage for him with its front paws. Its tail was wagging back and forth and it was trying to shake hands with him.

"He's got the saddest face I've ever seen," Quacky said.

"Most of the dogs in here have sad faces," the tall man replied. "Because no one wants them. They're all strays. Lost dogs. How about it? Want that one?"

The tall man took another dog out of its cage and began putting it into the cage with the others to be taken to the gas chamber.

"No," Quacky said. "I really don't want a mutt. I know my Aunt Maggie wouldn't let me bring a mutt into the house, anyway. It would just do things in the corners."

"You can housebreak a dog," Quacky was told. "So it'll do its duty outside."

"No, thanks, just the same. Come on, Ralph. Let's go."

As Quacky and Ralph turned to leave, they heard the little black puppy with the one white paw start to whimper. Quacky hesitated at the door. But again he reminded himself about what kind of dog he needed.

That's the difference, he realized. It was all a matter of who needed whom. He didn't need the mutt, but the mutt needed him. Just as he needed a real guardian. Someone like Jerry. But Jerry was a drifter. He didn't want responsibility, and he didn't need Quacky.

Quacky realized he and the little black pup were a lot alike. They both needed someone.

"You're not going to put that little pup to sleep today, are you?" he asked the tall man.

"Not today," the man replied. "But probably tomorrow. If no one wants him."

The pup was still standing on its hind legs. Its white paw was sticking out of the cage, and it seemed to be crying.

It's no use, Quacky told himself. I don't want a mutt, I *have* to have a show dog!

He left the building and he and Ralph and Clemontis Regis began walking home.

Quacky was sorry he ever went inside the dog pound. He kept seeing the little black pup with the white paw wherever he looked.

Until he had seen the pup, Quacky had been reasonably content to be on his own in the world. He had almost made a game out of taking care of himself, and not caring about not having anyone for a mother or father. Now the need for someone burned inside him. He decided he wanted that someone to be Jerry, bank robber or not. He *needed* Jerry, but how could he get Jerry to need *him*?

When they got near Aunt Maggie's house, Ralph took Clemontis Regis home. Quacky knocked on the kitchen door and Aunt Maggie let him in.

Jerry and Clem spread the newspaper out

on the kitchen table and looked at the front page. The headline, in big black type, read: "DARING BANK ROBBERS STILL AT BAY!"

"There's no bay around here," Quacky said.

"It means we're still missing," Jerry explained. "That's newspaper talk. Sometimes it's hard to understand."

" 'Police are checking out several clues,' " Clem read.

"But they don't say what they are," Jerry said. "I think they're bluffing. We didn't leave any clues behind."

" 'The robbers did not have a getaway car, but were on foot,' " Clem read on. " 'It is not known if they are still in Smedley or whether they stole a car and have left the area.' "

"And with the police chief living right next door!" Aunt Maggie chuckled.

"Who's living right next door?" Jerry asked.

"The chief of police," Aunt Maggie answered. "Didn't Quacky tell you?"

Quacky's face began to turn red. He hadn't told Jerry because he was afraid that if Jerry knew who lived next door, he would go for sure.

"And I thought we trusted each other," Jerry told Quacky.

81

"Ralph's father," Quacky informed him. "He's the police chief. But he's very nice. You'll like him."

"Oh, sure!" Clem said, looking very nervous. "I suppose we could all go bowling together!"

"He doesn't bowl, but he is into square dancing," Aunt Maggie replied. "He and his wife. We could *all* go square dancing tonight!"

"I know where *I'm* going!" Clem started for the stairs to the upstairs bedroom where he kept his things.

"Now hold on, Clem," Jerry told him. "Maybe we're not so bad off, hiding out right next door to the police chief. As long as he doesn't know we're here, it doesn't matter. We'll just have to make sure he doesn't know about us."

"We hardly ever see him," Quacky said. "He's always busy, out looking for some . . ."

"Criminal," Clem finished. "I say, let's go! While the going's good!"

"Not until we think this all out calmly," Jerry said. "Now that the police are out looking everywhere for us, it'd be harder to find another house to hide in. And maybe we'd find just as bad a situation there as here. Look at it this way, Clem . . . would the chief of police think of looking right next door for the bank robbers? Chances are it's the *last* place he'd look!"

"Chances are," Clem repeated, not as sure as Jerry.

" 'Bank officials still have not revealed what the valuable collection was that the robbers took,' " Quacky read from the newspaper.

"Old MacDougall must be sweating that one out," Jerry said. "It isn't a very long article. They just go on to describe what we were wearing. Remind me, if I do take a chance and leave the house, to change my clothes. Everyone in Smedley will be on the lookout for me in this shirt and you in that cream-colored suit, Clem."

"The paper says we're in for a heat wave," Aunt Maggie remarked. "The house will get pretty hot. You gentlemen will have to go out, to get relief. We have a lovely lake not far from town. You could go to the beach and take a swim," she suggested.

"I need fresh air," Jerry said, "to clear my head, so I can think. There are so many things I have to sort out. How about it, Quacky? We'll go for a swim!"

Quacky could think of nothing he would like better to do, especially with Jerry.

"I don't like the idea of you showing your

face around town," Clem told Jerry. "Someone might recognize you."

"We wore stocking masks," Jerry reminded him. "And I'll wear something else instead of this striped shirt and the white pants. Aunt Maggie, this may be a delicate question, but do you have any men's clothes around the house?"

"The question is 'delicate,' but as it happens, I *do* have some men's clothes," she said. She seemed to be deep in memories. "My last husband, Otis, was about your height and build."

"Your *last* husband?" Clem echoed. "How many came before him?"

"Otis was my fourth," Aunt Maggie said. "And then there was Buster. Oh, was he handsome! But there was never time for us to marry. Otis was the best, though. A real gentleman."

"What happened to Otis?" Jerry was interested.

"Walked out on me!" Aunt Maggie said, obviously still hurt about it. "It was in 1940. We went to the movies . . . the old Palace theater in Schenectady, where I was teaching English. He went out for popcorn and never came back. Right in the middle of *Gone With the Wind!*"

It was a sad story to Aunt Maggie but funny to the rest of them. She was so absorbed in thought, she didn't notice when they giggled.

"He was an Aquarius," Aunt Maggie said. "I should have known better. Aquarians take to just about everything but marriage. Poor Otis, he could stand it just so long. Then he vanished, like Rhett Butler. I divorced him after about seven years, when he didn't return."

Quacky led Jerry away before they would both break up. Clem went to the bathroom, where he could laugh in privacy.

Upstairs in Aunt Maggie's bedroom, Quacky showed Jerry Otis's clothes neatly hanging in a closet, waiting for the day he would return, with or without popcorn.

Jerry found a pair of old pants that reminded him of the 1940's, baggy and with large cuffs. And a faded shirt that was just a plain solid blue. It was a far cry from his fancy silk shirt, but he was glad to have it. Now no one would recognize him.

"Does she keep the clothes of all her ex-husbands?" Jerry asked, getting into Otis's shirt and pants.

"No, just Otis's," Quacky said. "The others took all their things before they left."

"You mean, all four walked out on her?" Jerry couldn't believe it.

"No," said Quacky. "Some of them *ran*!"

"How about a bathing suit for me?" Jerry asked.

Quacky rummaged through some bureau drawers and came up with a pair of baggy swim trunks. They were of a soft, shiny material with designs of beach balls all over them.

"I just hope we don't bump into Otis at the beach," Jerry remarked, taking the trunks and leading Quacky back downstairs. Clem was in the living room, watching television.

"Just be careful," Clem told Jerry.

"Before we go," Jerry said, "I want to take a look at that sewer."

Aunt Maggie showed Jerry the sewer near the house and he shook his head. "It's almost overflowing with gook," he said. "I'll have to figure a way of draining it. So I can find the outlet at the bottom and try to open it. You've probably got roots blocking the system."

"I have something Otis used to use to open it," Aunt Maggie told him. "It's a long wound-up thing. I don't remember what he called the nasty thing."

"It's probably a rodder," Jerry supplied. "A long metal rod with a knife on one end, for cutting the roots in the sewer line. Lucky you have one around the house. If we had to go out for one, someone might get suspicious. And speaking of someone getting suspicious, what are the neighbors going to think? Am I supposed to be the sewer repairman, or what?"

"You can be my nephew Roger, from Chicago," Aunt Maggie suggested. "I've mentioned him often, but no one around here has ever seen him. You could be visiting, with your friend."

"We'll have to take a chance on that, I guess. Just be sure you call me Roger if anyone comes by."

"I'll remember," Aunt Maggie assured him, and Quacky did too. "Now, what about groceries for lunch and dinner? Quacky can stay here as 'insurance,' while I go to the supermarket and do the shopping. But I need some money."

"How much do you need?" Jerry asked.

"I should think about twenty dollars would get us through lunch and dinner," she calculated.

"Figure just dinner for Quacky and me," Jerry said. "We'll probably be at the beach for lunch. There ought to be a hot-dog stand there."

Aunt Maggie went for her shopping cart

and purse and started to leave. Jerry called after her:

"Be sure to pay for everything you take!"

"Oh, I won't do any shoplifting," she said. "I wouldn't want to bring the police back here."

"You just be sure you don't," Clem warned from the television set. "Or we'll take it out on Quacky."

"Don't let him frighten you," Jerry told Quacky. "He wouldn't do anything to you. At least, I don't think he'd try. And if he did, I wouldn't let him."

After Aunt Maggie left, Clem opened all the windows. It was getting very hot in the house and she kept the windows closed, to keep out the dust. Clem was very frustrated. He had enough money to buy a dozen air conditioners and have them delivered and installed, but he couldn't because it would attract attention to them. He went back to his television set and opened another can of beer. Watching the baseball game on a tiny set with a round screen and the figures all tall as Zulu warriors nearly drove him crazy.

"What can we do while Aunt Maggie's gone?" Jerry asked. "It's too hot to start work on the sewer."

"How about a game of poker?'" Quacky suggested.

"My favorite card game," Jerry said.

"It's what kept me going, in the orphanages," Quacky said.

"It kept me going, on the road," Jerry said.

While they played, Quacky heard a noise from out front. Jerry told Quacky he could check on it, but to be careful.

Quacky went out the front door and looked around, but did not see anyone. He heard the noise again: a soft, whimpering sound. Looking down, he saw a small black puppy with one white paw. He stooped down, took the puppy in his arms, and stroked it. The pup stopped crying and licked his hands.

"Oh no, you don't!" Quacky said. "You're not gonna make me get soft-hearted about you and take you in. No way! It's a pair of pedigree Basenji I'm after. Cute as you are, little fellow. How'd you get here?"

He was about to put the pup back down and make him scoot when he saw a panel truck with lettering on the side: "City Dog Pound." The two men he had talked with at the pound earlier that morning were getting out of the truck and coming up the front walk.

"He got away from us," the tall man explained. "When we were putting him into another cage."

"I thought you said you wouldn't put him to sleep until tomorrow or later," Quacky reminded him.

"We're just getting too crowded," the tall man replied. "I'm afraid it's today for this mutt."

"I just changed my mind!" Quacky held the puppy close. *"I'll* take him! Is he still going to cost five dollars?"

"Keep him, with our compliments." The tall man smiled. "He's had his shots. Just keep him on a leash when you take him out. Until you get his name tag. When you come up with a name for him. He was lost and didn't have a name."

"Well, you're not lost now," Quacky told the mutt.

The men left in their panel truck and Quacky waited until they were gone before going inside the house.

"Who was out there?" Jerry followed Quacky into the kitchen. "What do you have there?"

"Just someone else on the run from the law," Quacky said, holding up the puppy for Jerry to see.

A DOG'S LIFE

"What was I going to do?" Quacky asked Aunt Maggie when she came back from shopping and saw he had taken in another stray. "They were going to gas the little guy. And they were practically inside the house before I could stop them by agreeing to take the dog."

"Oh, so he's our fault." Jerry was amused.

"If he messes in any of my corners, out he goes!" Aunt Maggie warned Quacky.

"He is a cute fellow." Jerry stroked the puppy's head.

"Me, I can do without dogs," Clem said. "But I don't think we'll be staying here much longer, so it don't matter."

Quacky looked at Clem. He wished Clem wouldn't keep saying that he and Jerry would not be staying much longer. He looked at Jerry and got a little reassurance.

"We'll be here for a while, anyway," Jerry told Quacky.

Quacky cuddled the mutt and asked for ideas for a name.

"Bowser," Clem suggested. "I've heard that dogs are supposed to be called Bowser, but I've never heard a dog called that."

"Doesn't fit him," Quacky said. He set the puppy down on the kitchen floor and no sooner did the dog's paws touch ground than he wet enough to mess up half the floor.

Aunt Maggie wailed and ran for a mop.

"Puddles," said Quacky. "He's named himself!"

"If he does that again, he's going to make his puddles outside," Aunt Maggie warned.

Clem went back to watching the baseball game and fell asleep. Jerry said he was going upstairs to try on Otis's bathing trunks. If they fit, he told them, he and Quacky would go swimming.

Jerry came downstairs a few minutes later with the trunks on under his pants and he and Quacky and Puddles went to the beach. Clem stayed at home with Aunt Maggie and tried to breathe in the hot house with the windows closed again. Aunt Maggie insisted that she had to keep the dust out.

The beach was crowded, but Jerry was glad. The more people, the better, because he would be lost in the crowd. They had taken a bus to get to the lake and Jerry was hot and tired. He couldn't wait to take a swim and cool off.

They found a patch of sand where they put down their towels. It was off to one side of the beach, in an area where dogs were allowed. Puddles watched them swim, from the safety of the shallow water. Then they lay down on their towels to get some sun, and Puddles curled up on the edge of Quacky's towel and took a long nap.

"Wouldn't it be great if we could do this every day?" Quacky asked. He looked at Jerry beside him, his eyes closed.

"Can't ever count on doing what you'd like to do every day," Jerry replied. "But it would be nice to do this."

"You know what I wish?" Quacky asked.

"No, what?"

Quacky decided not to tell. What he really

wished was that Jerry would stay around for good.

They had hot dogs and Cokes for lunch on the beach and Jerry even bought one for Puddles, who had his dog plain. Afterward they soaked up some more sun and talked, about the money Jerry and Clem had stolen from the bank.

"Why *don't* you return all but a couple of hundred dollars of the money?" Quacky asked. He sat Indian-style on his beach towel, Puddles napping again on one corner. "Then maybe the police wouldn't be after you and Clem and you could both be free men again."

"We'd still not be free men," Jerry said, lying on his back and enjoying the sun on him. "We'd still be bank robbers, no matter how much we stole."

"But stealing a couple hundred isn't anywhere near as serious as stealing a hundred thousand, is it?"

"To the law, stealing anything is serious, especially with a gun. See what a bad influence I am on you? I've got you thinking you can go around robbing banks and it's okay, if you just steal a little."

"But if you give back the money, you could get the reward," Quacky pointed out.

"They don't give reward money to bank robbers." Suddenly Jerry sat up. "That's it!" he said, reaching out and thumping Quacky on the back. "*You'll* return the money! All but a few hundred, which Clem and I will need to get started again, away from Smedley. And you and Aunt Maggie will get the thousand-dollar reward for finding the stolen money. And, hey! You can return the toy soldiers too! And collect another grand from old Mac-Dougall!"

Quacky could hardly follow it, Jerry was making plans so fast.

Jerry got up and began putting on his clothes over his swim suit.

"We've got to talk this all out back at the house and see how Clem takes to the plan," Jerry said.

"I don't think he's gonna like it much," Quacky replied.

When they got back to the house, it was full of ladies, all talking at once.

"My bridge club," Aunt Maggie explained to Jerry. "It meets here every Wednesday, except when I'm in jail."

Jerry looked at Clem. "How'd you let them in?" he asked.

"How could I keep them out?" Clem threw

up his arms. "You think I've been able to follow the baseball game, with all the cackling going on?"

"But aren't they curious?" Jerry asked. "About who you are?"

Aunt Maggie left her ladies for a moment and took Jerry aside. "Don't worry, come with me."

She led Jerry into the dining room, where four card tables and chairs were set up and four ladies sat at each table. She called for their attention, but they were too busy talking, so she made her announcement anyway.

"Girls, I'd like you to meet my nephew Roger, from Detroit."

"I'm supposed to be from Chicago, I think," Jerry whispered.

"From Chicago!" Aunt Maggie corrected herself. "And his friend. I forgot his name. Go on playing girls. There's plenty of cold beer in the icebox."

None of the ladies looked her way while Aunt Maggie introduced Jerry and Clem. They were too occupied dealing out cards and talking.

"Go ahead, get in the game," Jerry told her. "Just get rid of them as soon as you can."

"They've only just arrived," Aunt Maggie

said. "If I throw them out, they're bound to get suspicious. I expect they'll be here all afternoon. Do you play bridge?"

"I wouldn't if I did!" Jerry said, going to the kitchen for a beer. He saw Clem in his chair in the living room, hunched over and trying to concentrate on the ball game.

Jerry brought his beer into the living room and pulled a chair up next to Clem. He explained what he was thinking about back at the beach. Quacky sat on the floor and played with Puddles.

"Oh no you don't," Clem told Jerry. "I knew the kid and his daffy aunt would get to you. I'm not for giving back a cent of what we took, or the soldiers. We're wanted bank robbers, no matter how much we stole or how much we give back. It's crazy to even give back a dollar of the money or any of the soldiers."

"But the reward money will be plenty for both of us," Jerry insisted. "And we can be free men again."

"I figure you'll give half the reward money to the kid and his aunt," Clem said. "Or maybe all of it! And the only way for us to be 'free men' again is to give ourselves up. But even then we wouldn't be free until after we got out of jail, in twenty or thirty years, if we're lucky. I don't know about you, but I got no ants in my pants for going to jail!"

"Maybe I could think this out some more," said Jerry. "If only I could find some peace and quiet around this crazy house."

"If you find it, you tell me where it is." Clem went back to watching the ball game.

"Quacky, you want to watch me drain a sewer?" The only way to escape the bridge ladies was to get out of the house and work on the sewer, Jerry decided.

Quacky followed him out into the back yard with Puddles.

"I never knew before how nice silence sounds!" Jerry said. He asked Quacky where Aunt Maggie kept the tools around the house, and found the sewer rodder Otis had left behind years ago. Jerry rolled up his sleeves and began poking around in the sewer.

It wound up that Jerry had to drain the whole sewer before he could rod the line out, and Quacky had to help. Jerry got buckets full of smelly water and muck out of the sewer. Quacky emptied the buckets in the alley one by one. It took about an hour, but Jerry said it was better than being inside with the bridge ladies.

"It is pretty funny, though." Jerry stopped a minute to wipe his forehead. "Here I am, sloshing around in an old sewer, with fifty thousand dollars in my pockets!"

When the sewer was finally drained, Jerry reported the good news to Aunt Maggie. She was in the kitchen, preparing a late afternoon snack for the bridge ladies.

"You know, Aunt Maggie, that's the first real work I've done in about a year," Jerry said. "And it feels good!"

"But you don't smell so good," she told him. "Why don't you take a nice long shower upstairs. I'll be working on trying to get the ladies out. And Quacky, smells to me like you could use a shower too."

Jerry and Quacky took turns in the shower and when they came back to the kitchen, Aunt Maggie was in another uproar about Puddles. He had wet all over the kitchen floor again.

"He stays in the kitchen now," she told Quacky. "Until he learns to do it outside. I don't want him wetting on my good rugs."

Jerry opened a can of beer and they heard Ralph again out in the back yard, calling for Quacky.

"Don't let him in!" Jerry warned. "Talk to him from the door, but make it short. The police chief's son!" He shook his head. "Good grief!"

Quacky talked to Ralph through the kitchen screen door while Jerry stood out of sight.

"My folks want you and Aunt Maggie to join us in the yard tonight, for a candlelight cookout," Ralph said. "There'll be a few others. How about it?"

"I'll have to ask Aunt Maggie."

Aunt Maggie was serving tiny sandwiches with shrimp and herring and nuts and cheese on small pieces of bread, in the dining room with the bridge ladies when Quacky told her what Ralph came for. She told Jerry.

"They'll be suspicious if I refuse," she said. "I never refuse. The chief always serves a choice cut of steak. Why don't we all accept his invitation? I'll just introduce you and Clem as I did to my bridge ladies."

"Even for a steak dinner, that's pretty risky," Jerry told her. "My teeth might chatter, sitting there eating dinner with the chief of police!"

"He's sure to come over here if I say no," Aunt Maggie pointed out. "He'll ask about my health and all sorts of things."

Jerry told Clem about it and Clem nearly dropped his beer can.

"Are you crazy?" he asked Jerry. "We can't get away with any stunt as looney as that! Having dinner with the chief of police! Jerry, the sun must have got to you!"

"Will the chief really come here, if we don't go there?" Jerry asked Aunt Maggie.

"Sure as Thursday follows Wednesday," she said.

"Then tell him you accept," Jerry said. "We *all* accept."

Clem slouched in his chair and groaned.

"That's swell!" Ralph was pleased when Quacky informed him the four of them would come to the cook-out. "And hey, did you hear the news? That bank president just upped the reward money for the mysterious collection to *two* thousand dollars! Everybody in town is out treasure hunting, hoping to find the metal box. If it's still somewhere around Smedley."

"Thanks for the news," Quacky said. Then he remembered Puddles and told Ralph about him.

"Thought you were going to raise Basenji show dogs," Ralph said.

"Maybe I still will. But you know, I'm getting pretty attached to the mutt. I'd let you see him, but I've got some chores. See you later."

Quacky didn't have to tell the others the news. They had overheard Ralph.

"Old MacDougall must be getting antsy," said Aunt Maggie. "Afraid someone's going to let it out about his toy soldiers."

"Maggie, aren't you coming in to play a hand?" one of the ladies called from the dining room.

"Get rid of those women!" Jerry ordered.

Puddles did it again. This time he wet nowhere near the newspaper Quacky had put by the kitchen door.

"That does it!" Aunt Maggie decided. "Out in the back yard with him! He eats, sleeps, and lives outside from now on!"

"Maybe you can help me build him a doghouse," Quacky suggested to Jerry.

"Good idea," Jerry said. "It'll keep us busy until Aunt Maggie gets rid of the ladies."

They found enough odds and ends of lumber for a doghouse and the project kept Jerry occupied. When he had the walls and roof assembled, he showed Quacky how to nail it all together.

"It's a nice doghouse," Quacky remarked after finishing the job. "Puddles, this is your new home."

"Quieter than ours," Jerry said.

Puddles went right inside and curled up to take another nap.

"How did Clem take it, about your plan to return the money and the soldiers?" Quacky asked Jerry.

"About as I expected," Jerry replied. "He wants no part of it. Quacky, I don't want to frighten you, but I think Clem might use his gun on me if I tried giving up the money or the toys. I guess he doesn't care as much as I do about being a fugitive. I sure wish I'd never gone into that bank with him. We were flat broke and we had to do something to eat, so Clem said we ought to rob the bank. 'Just take five hundred dollars,' he told me. And I was dumb enough to let him talk me into it."

A summer rainstorm began building up. It finally drove the ladies out.

"I can't get my hair wet!" one said.

"I have a new dress on!" said another.

One by one, they left and when they were gone, Jerry collapsed into a chair.

Quacky talked Aunt Maggie into letting Puddles back into the house during the rainstorm. "He'd get awfully scared of the thunder and lightning," he said.

"Just so he stays in the kitchen," she warned. "If he leaves this room, he goes back outside."

Quacky hoped it would rain all night. Then Puddles could stay in the house with him.

"Someone's at the front door," Aunt Maggie said. "Maybe one of my bridge-club ladies forgot something."

"Whoever it is, get *rid* of them!" Jerry wailed.

Aunt Maggie opened the door. "Why Reverend Du Vall!" She let in a short, thin man in a black suit with a white collar.

Jerry could not protest or the preacher would get suspicious. So he just sat and wondered what was happening.

"I told you we should get out of here!" Clem whispered to Jerry. "Now the Church is after us!"

"I've two foreign missionaries from India with me," the preacher said. He held the door open and two tall, thin men wearing orange-colored bed sheets and sandals came in. "I've placed others in friends' homes for a few days. But I need a temporary home for these two good religious men."

"Of course, Reverend," Aunt Maggie said. "I've never turned away any of your nice missionaries. These two are different, though, aren't they?"

"Many persuasions, one God," Reverend DuVall said. "Bless you, sister. I'll just leave them with you. By the way, this is Sumanji and this is Narguru."

Quacky couldn't tell them apart.

"Oh, by the way," Reverend DuVall said upon leaving. "They don't speak English. But they'll only be staying a week." He went away.

"Get rid of them!" Jerry whispered angrily to Aunt Maggie. "Farm them out to someone else. Try the Salvation Army, but get *rid* of them!"

"I'll do what I can," Aunt Maggie whispered back and turned to the missionaries. "I don't have room for you. I'm sorry, but you must go."

They bowed and smiled and shook her hand.

"They don't understand," Aunt Maggie told Jerry, looking at him helplessly. "What if I find a place for them in the attic?"

Jerry threw out his arms hopelessly. He went to the kitchen for a fresh beer.

"Hey!" Clem followed Jerry to the refrigerator. "Who are the two dudes in the orange bed sheets?"

"They're going to live in the attic for a

week," Jerry explained. He seemed resigned to the fact. "At least they don't speak any English. So they won't know what we're doing here or what we're saying."

The missionaries came into the kitchen. They used sign language to indicate they would both like something to drink too.

"They're gonna be trouble," Clem said. "I can tell."

The rain continued for some time. Aunt Maggie was sure it would keep the police chief from going through with his cook-out. But then, the rain finally stopped. The chief's wife telephoned Aunt Maggie to say the cook-out was still on.

"What'll I wear?" Jerry asked. "These old things of Otis's make me look like I stepped out of a 1940 time capsule!"

"I'm sure I can find something suitable for a cook-out among Otis's things," Aunt Maggie told him. "Otis, for all his faults, was quite a dapper dresser."

"What about me?" Clem asked. "Unless I can be excused. I do think I have a headache."

"You're coming too," Jerry told him. "If I have to go through this, so do you!"

"And what about the missionaries?" asked Clem.

Aunt Maggie replied, "They won't be going. Sumanji and Narguru signaled they are vegetarians. I've got salad and fruit in the icebox for them.

"Otis put on some weight late in our marriage." Aunt Maggie was again deep in memories. "It was around the time we saw *The Wizard of Oz*, and I remember thinking he looked like quite a large Munchkin. I've saved some of his things from when he was heavier. I'm sure I can fit you into something nice, Clem."

She rummaged through Otis's closet and came up with several outfits for Jerry and Clem. A small fashion show was held in her bedroom as they changed from one shirt and pants into another.

Jerry finally settled on a pair of white Navy-type bell-bottom trousers Otis had come by somehow, and a short-sleeve shirt he had bought years ago in Hawaii.

"All I need is a ukulele," Jerry said.

"Oh, do you play?" Aunt Maggie asked. "I have one!"

"Forget it!" Jerry told her.

Clem managed to get into some old brown suit pants that had been too small for Otis but which Clem could keep on him, if he didn't breathe too deeply. His shirt was a striped pullover with short sleeves that choked him at the neck.

"If I don't have to eat or talk or sit down or breathe, I think I'll make it," he said.

Aunt Maggie had changed into a party dress she said she had worn at a reception for her and her second husband. It was a long, trailing gown of shocking pink. She wore it with four strands of imitation pearls, the silver high-heels, and a billowy feather affair in purple, which she wore around her neck and down the back.

Quacky came in his frayed blue jeans and blue football jersey with the "38" across the chest. Aunt Maggie had tried to get him to dress up, but he threatened to run away from home.

The chief of police, a heavyset man of Clem's age named Dooley, waved them into his yard which was aglow with candlelight. He was wearing his yachting outfit of white pants and shoes with a blue blazer and captain's cap. Mrs. Dooley, a small, stout woman, wore a pantsuit of bright yellow that clashed with Aunt Maggie's pink and purple.

Aunt Maggie introduced Jerry and Clem as her houseguests, remembering to say they were visitors from Chicago. Chief Dooley shook hands with them.

The steaks were sizzling on Chief Dooley's grill. Beside him was a punch bowl. Jerry warned Quacky to stay away from it since it had been liberally spiked with vodka.

"How are things in Chicago?" the chief asked Jerry. "I used to live there, on Sheridan Road near the lake."

"They're both still there." Jerry quickly changed the subject, never having been in Chicago. "So you sail . . ."

The subject of sailing kept Chief Dooley occupied for some time.

"And where did you say you're from?" a man asked Clem. He had introduced himself as Dennis Fabian, chief of the robbery detail of the Smedley police department.

"I thought I would die!" Quacky heard Clem tell Jerry later that night, after the cook-out, when they were getting ready for bed. "I could hardly keep my voice from cracking. The pants and shirt were killing me. Then this cop in charge of the robbery detail starts pumping me for details about who I am and where I came from. I tell you, Jerry, we were nuts to try and get away with a stunt like that! If they didn't catch on to us, they're dumber than they looked!"

"If they had suspected us, we wouldn't be here now," Jerry scoffed. He yawned and stretched in his shorts and made himself comfortable on the mattress on the floor in Quacky's room. "I'm exhausted. What a day! And I drained a sewer and built a doghouse besides! I haven't worked this hard in my life!"

Quacky smiled as he curled up between Jerry and Clem where the two mattresses met. He was content. Since it had started raining again, Aunt Maggie agreed to let Puddles sleep in the house that night.

When he was sure everyone was asleep, Quacky crept downstairs. He found Puddles in the kitchen and brought him back upstairs. The mutt slept at Quacky's feet and Quacky finally fell happily asleep.

ON THE RUN

Quacky awakened early in the morning. He saw that Jerry and Clem were still asleep. An idea came to him just then and he was very excited about it.

Quietly, so as not to awaken them, Quacky got up and tiptoed to the chair where Jerry had laid his white pants and striped shirt and Clem his cream-colored suit. Then he got his own clothes from another chair.

Carrying all the clothes over one arm, he lifted Puddles up with his free hand and tiptoed down the stairs to the kitchen, where he dressed.

A wonderful plan was jelling in his head and he wished he could tell someone about it.

But he knew he couldn't take a chance on telling Aunt Maggie. She might wake up Jerry and Clem. And it was too early in the morning for Ralph to be up, so Quacky could not tell him. Besides, he hadn't told Ralph who Jerry and Clem really were. With Ralph's father being Smedley's chief of police, Quacky could not take a chance revealing his secret to his best friend.

Quacky took Jerry's and Clem's clothes and Puddles and quietly left the house. Out in the back yard he found his bicycle chained to a tree. He worked the combination lock and unchained the bike, then carefully rolled Jerry's white pants and striped shirt into a package and put it on one side of his twin wire baskets, over the rear wheel. Then he rolled the cream-colored suit into a package and placed it in the other wire basket. Lastly, he put Puddles in the wicker basket on the handlebars, patted his head, and walked the bike out the back gate.

He pedaled up the alley and over to a main crosstown street. Only a milk truck passed him as he rolled along in the early light of day.

On he rode for about five miles, until he was deep into the opposite end of Smedley. He could see the neighborhood was very poor and Quacky felt a little unsafe being alone in it, especially so early in the morning. Some people were up now, walking the streets and standing on corners at bus stops. They were dressed in shabby clothes and some even looked mean to him. He worried that someone might even try to steal his bicycle.

Finally he rode his bike into the parking lot of a supermarket. The market was not yet open, but a few trucks had stopped near the service entrances. Men were unloading things from the trucks for the store people to sell that day.

He pedaled past the trucks and at last found what he had come all that way to find: a Salvation Army drop-off box. He got off his bike, took the white pants, striped shirt, and cream-colored suit and tossed them into the box.

"There!" he said, wiping his hands off. "Now my plan will go into action!"

Quacky pulled his bike into the back yard and carried Puddles into the house with him. He found Jerry and Clem in the kitchen where Aunt Maggie was serving them breakfast. They were wearing some more old clothes that Uncle Otis had left behind.

"Okay, kid, where did you put my suit?" Clem asked, looking up from his plate.

"And my pants and shirt?" Jerry added. "There was nothing in the pockets, was there?"

"I checked them before I left the house with them," Quacky told them both. "I wouldn't steal anything from you."

"What about our clothes you took?" Clem asked. "Ain't that stealing?"

Quacky told them about his plan. It would throw the police off their trail.

"I tossed your clothes into a Salvation Army pick-up box all the way across town," Quacky said. "Whoever finds them and wears them will be picked up as the bank robbers."

"Not a bad plan," Jerry admitted. "But what happens when whoever wears our clothes says they didn't rob the bank? Maybe they can prove they were somewhere else at the time of the robbery."

"Then," said Quacky, "the police put two and two together. They figure that the real bank robbers got as far as that part of Smedley after the robbery. And then they dumped their clothes into the Salvation Army box to get rid of them. The police will figure the robbers put on other clothes for the rest of their escape and probably left town!"

"The kid's a good detective," Clem observed to Jerry. "I think he's helped throw the cops off our trail. At least for a while."

"Okay, Quacky," Jerry said. "That was a pretty neat trick. Only, next time, ask us about it first, okay?"

"I'm sorry I had to toss away your favorite shirt," Quacky told Jerry as he sat down at the table for Aunt Maggie's pancakes.

"There are more where that came from," Jerry replied. "All in all, I think it was a pretty good idea."

After breakfast, Aunt Maggie started in about her gutters.

"I'm just worried that city inspector's going to come out here today," she said. "If she sees I haven't done anything yet about scraping and painting my gutters, she'll fine me and probably make all kinds of trouble."

"She?" Clem asked. "Your city inspector's a woman?"

"Clem," Aunt Maggie replied, "this *is* the twentieth century, you know! Welcome to Women's Lib!"

"I guess I just never expected them to get

into that kind of work." Clem shook his head over his pancakes.

"How about it, Clem?" Jerry asked. "We don't have anything better to do today. Suppose we fix up Aunt Maggie's gutters?"

Clem mumbled into his coffee.

"Swell!" Jerry laughed. "You'll love it! Aunt Maggie, you got a couple of high ladders? And we'll need some scraping brushes and some paint."

"It's all in the basement. I called the hardware store for it all yesterday, and put it on the bill. You did such a good job on my sewer, Jerry, I figured I could trust you with my gutters."

Jerry looked at her. "Thanks a lot."

Clem was still mumbling and grumbling when he and Jerry began to work on the gutters after breakfast. Quacky figured that what was riling him up more than anything was that Sumanji and Narguru were both squatting on the grass chanting and clanging their cymbals while Jerry and Clem worked.

Aunt Maggie whispered to Quacky, "Jerry's kind of worried about Clem. While you were away this morning and Clem was in the shower, Jerry said he's afraid Clem wants to take off. With his half of the money and the

116

toy collection. But Jerry wants to stay with us at least a few days more. He's sure it's safer here than trying to leave town."

"Wonder how we can be sure Clem won't leave?" Quacky asked.

"I'm sure that between us, we can think of a way to keep him from leaving," Aunt Maggie assured him.

While she busied herself doing the breakfast dishes, Quacky fed Puddles in the back yard by his doghouse. Afterward, while Jerry and Clem were busy preparing the paint to do the gutters, Quacky checked out the ladders for them. Aunt Maggie had bought one new one, but the other was an old one that had been around the house for years. The new one was of shiny aluminum, very strong and sturdy. The old one was of wood. It looked a little unsafe. The fourth rung was very wobbly. Too heavy a weight might break it.

Quacky hoped that Jerry would be using the aluminum ladder, and that Clem would get the wooden one. He didn't want anything to happen to Jerry. He had faith that Jerry would outfox Clem for it.

Puddles cuddled in Quacky's lap as he sat on the grass with the missionaries and watched Jerry and Clem debate over who was to get to use the new ladder. Just as Quacky expected, Jerry stuck Clem with the old one.

Quacky watched with his mouth open as Clem started climbing the ladder. Clem's weight caused the bottom of the old wooden ladder to sink into the lawn a few inches where he had it set up on one side of the house.

Clem stepped on the first rung, then the second, then the third. Quacky's heart beat faster as Clem stepped up to the fourth rung.

But it held his weight, to Quacky's surprise and disappointment. Clem stepped up the ladder to the fifth rung and then climbed up to near the top where he began scraping the gutters under the roof.

The sun grew hotter as the morning wore on, and each time Clem came down from the ladder and went up it again, Quacky watched with his heart in his mouth. But each time Clem moved the ladder, he made it safely up and down.

Quacky grew more concerned as Clem worked harder in the hot sun. Clem was complaining more and more to Jerry that they were crazy to be working so hard on someone else's house, when they had a fortune in their pockets. They should take off and start having themselves a good time!

After a few hours, someone called up to Jerry from below.

"That's sure being nice to your Aunt Maggie, on such a hot day!"

Jerry looked down from his ladder and saw that it was Chief of Police Dooley, next door.

"They sure need painting!" Jerry replied, turning back to his work.

Chief Dooley sat in his back yard and drank a cup of coffee as he watched Jerry and Clem work.

"After you're finished on Aunt Maggie's gutters," he told Clem, "you can do mine!"

It was an old joke, and Clem thought it was even less funny coming from the police chief under the circumstances.

Aunt Maggie called the men down from their ladders shortly before noon for lunch. Quacky watched again anxiously as Clem came down his ladder. But again the fourth rung held his weight.

"How about trading ladders this afternoon?" Clem asked Jerry. "No thanks, I'm used to mine," replied Jerry. Quacky was very relieved.

Jerry and Clem wanted to watch the noon

news on TV, so Aunt Maggie served their lunches by the set. Quacky and Aunt Maggie watched, too.

"Police report an interesting development this morning in the daring bank robbery of two days ago," the TV newsman said.

Everyone but the missionaries and Puddles sat closer and listened more intently.

"Two men were arrested a short time ago on the far south side of town," the newsman went on. "They had held up a gas station, robbed the owner of fifty dollars, and then taken his car. They attempted to rob the South Smedley Federal Bank but were apprehended while leaving the bank when a guard surprised them.

"Police investigating the attempted robbery said the two men were dressed in the identical clothes worn by the robbers in the earlier bank robbery two days ago. One wore a cream-colored suit and the other white pants and a striped shirt.

"At this time, both men deny robbing the other bank and also taking the valuable collection, which still remains a mystery. They told police that they found the clothes in a Salvation Army box near the gas station they admit to robbing. Police now are attempting to check out their story. But Lieutenant Dennis Fabian, chief of the robbery detail, said he believes the two men did find the clothing. He does not think they are the same men who robbed the First National Bank of Smedley two days ago. Lieutenant Fabian suspects those bank robbers are still in town."

The newsman then turned to a story of a man who was arrested at the beach near Smedley, wearing just tattoos from head to toe.

"Well, that will keep them busy for a while," Clem said. "But I'm for going *now*! What better time, since they're all wrapped up questioning those two other guys?"

"Now's the worst time to leave Aunt Maggie's," Jerry objected. "If the police don't think those two guys robbed our bank, they'll be wondering how those clothes of ours got into that Salvation Army box. And *when*."

Clem looked at Quacky. "You better not pull another stunt like that again!"

"Leave the boy alone," Jerry said. "He was only trying to help. And I don't think he's done any harm. So long as no one saw him dump off the clothes."

"No one was around," Quacky assured him. "I was very careful about nobody seeing me."

"Then it's okay," Jerry said.

"No more gutters for me," Clem said. "The baseball game will be on soon. I've got the game explained pretty well so far to those two gurus in the bedsheets."

"How can you make them understand?" Aunt Maggie asked. "They don't speak a word of English."

"I use sign language," Clem explained. He started to show them how he demonstrated someone pitching, at bat, and running bases.

"Someone's at the back door," Quacky said, hearing a noise.

Jerry and Clem looked anxiously at each other.

"Be careful, Aunt Maggie." Jerry nodded his head for her to go see who was there.

Chief of Police Dooley's wife called to Aunt Maggie. "Oh, Maggie, I'm so upset. I've just heard the most awful news . . ."

"Let's go!" Clem whispered, grabbing Jerry by an arm.

"Wait, shhh!" Jerry said. "Let's hear . . ."

"Oh, it's just so terrible," Mrs. Dooley said, almost in tears.

Aunt Maggie let her in and she sat in a kitchen chair and sobbed.

"I just got a phone call from my brother

Argus in Idaho," Mrs. Dooley said. "His wife has gone off and left him! And they were married for almost thirty years!"

"The poor man," Aunt Maggie soothed Mrs. Dooley. "I know just how he feels."

"I've asked him to come here and stay with us," Mrs. Dooley told her. "He's going to take the first plane he can. Maybe you can help comfort him. I mean, you've had such experience, Maggie."

"What's his sign?" Aunt Maggie asked.

"Why, he's an Aquarius. Is that a good sign?"

Aunt Maggie was thinking. An Aquarius . . . same sign as Otis. Her eyes lit up.

"I think it's a very good sign," she said. "What is your brother like?"

"Oh, he's a darling," Mrs. Dooley smiled. "He's about your age, I should think. Very good-looking and very healthy. He loves poetry and he's really a romantic, sentimental dear."

Quacky listened to them talking, and ran out to tell Jerry he thought Aunt Maggie was ready to fall in love again.

"Okay, Clem," Jerry was saying. "You can get out of helping with the gutters this afternoon. But first clean up your mess out there. And put your ladder away."

Clem told Sumanji and Narguru he would be right back to watch baseball with them. He went into the back yard while Jerry took Quacky aside.

"We've got to find a way to keep Clem here," Jerry said. "He's got ants in his pants to start running. But we're doing fine here. Got any ideas?"

"Ahhhhh!" An awful cry from the back yard filled the air. Everyone rushed out to see what was the matter.

Clem lay on the ground beneath the old wooden ladder. He was holding his right leg and cursing the ladder. The fourth rung from the bottom was broken into two pieces.

"I think my leg's broken," he told them.

Jerry looked at Quacky and Quacky looked at Jerry. "I guess we'll be here a little longer," Jerry said.

Aunt Maggie said she had been a nurse in her younger days and knew a sprain from a break when she saw one. There would be no need to call a doctor or take Clem to a hospital.

"Good thing," Jerry said. "A doctor asks a lot of questions. Can you fix him up so he can stay here, Aunt Maggie?"

"He'll be fine in about a week," she said. "But he has to stay off his feet. I can fix him up so he can sit up in a chair and watch his baseball game."

Clem groaned and cursed as Jerry and Quacky helped carry him into the house and put him into the chair he sat in to watch television. Aunt Maggie went for her first-aid kit and began wrapping up his ankle.

While Clem was resting comfortably with his right ankle in a bandage, watching baseball, Aunt Maggie poured coffee for Jerry in the kitchen. Quacky sat with them and listened as they talked.

"Clem won't agree to give back the money or the toy collection," Jerry told her. "I think he'd use his gun on anyone who tried giving back either."

Aunt Maggie was busy with books and papers and charts she had spread out on the table.

"I wish I knew Clem's sign," she said. "We would know a lot more about him. But he won't tell me. He doesn't believe in astrology. But that doesn't bother me. I've been studying him and believe he's a Scorpio. He's not a romantic, he's much more interested in money. Scorpios are very loyal to friends, though. So you shouldn't worry that he'll turn on you, Jerry."

"I hope your reading is right about that," he replied.

"Scorpios are very possessive about what they feel belongs to them," Aunt Maggie went on. "Just be careful with him. Because Scorpios are good at solving mysteries. Clem will suspect what you may be plotting, if you're plotting against him. Then beware, because a Scorpio won't rest until he settles a score and gets things back to being his way again."

"Sounds like Clem all right," Jerry sighed. "How about a daily horoscope? A prediction about my day coming up?"

Aunt Maggie consulted her charts.

"This is a day for big decisions for Geminis. You have a lot to win, but a lot to lose too. Be careful where affairs of the heart are concerned."

"How about Clem's day?" Jerry asked.

"Scorpios," Aunt Maggie said, laughing, "will have an up and down day. One thing is for certain . . . travel is bad for him today."

Ralph called from outside for Quacky and he left the kitchen. Then the front doorbell rang and Jerry nodded to Aunt Maggie to answer it.

A young woman stood at the door, holding a purse and a black briefcase.

"I'm sorry," Aunt Maggie told her, trying to close the door on her. "But I already gave to the March of Dimes. And to the Red Cross and Community Fund and Cancer Society and the Diabetes Foundation. I already read all the literature for the Temple of God Followers someone else came around with last month, and I can't afford any more insurance or magazines."

"I'm from the Smedley Police Department." The young lady showed a badge. "I'm Lieutenant O'Rourke of the felony squad. I've been assigned to your case."

"I didn't know I had a case," Aunt Maggie replied. "Or that I was one."

"It's about your . . . Well, you know . . . the things you take from supermarkets now and then," Lieutenant O'Rourke explained. "May I come in?"

Aunt Maggie had no choice. She had to let the policewoman enter before Jerry could escape to the basement.

"This is my nephew, from Chicago," Aunt Maggie said, introducing Jerry to the policewoman. "And that's his friend there in the living room, watching baseball!"

Jerry looked surprised, seeing a police-woman. Lieutenant O'Rourke noticed and smiled.

"I hope you're not a male chauvinist," she told him. "Women *do* have their places in society, you know."

He thought she was very pretty, in a businesslike sort of way. She had short-cut brown hair and deep blue eyes, and her figure looked very nice in her blue policewoman's uniform.

"Oh, I'm all for women," Jerry said. "Working, I mean. In society, of course."

"Well, I'm glad to meet at least one man who is," she said.

Lieutenant O'Rourke got down to business and asked Aunt Maggie about her experiences as a shoplifter. Aunt Maggie explained in great detail how her Social Security did not allow her to live anywhere near what she, a Leo, had the natural taste for. So she had been forced to make up for it by shoplifting.

After an hour, Lieutenant O'Rourke finished filling out several long forms on Aunt Maggie. She also finished asking all the question she could think of and several others that Aunt Maggie suggested the policewoman ask.

"I think I can safely say I won't be shoplifting anymore," Aunt Maggie assured her.

"My chart says I'm coming into some money." She managed not to look at Jerry when she said that.

"Well, I hope your chart is right," Lieutenant O'Rourke replied. "But if it should be wrong, I hope you'll simply do without, the next time you get a craving for pickled eggplant or a small ham and a six-pack of beer, and you haven't the money to pay for them at the checkout counter. Think of your nephew. He sounds like quite a nice boy. I must warn you . . . if you're caught once more, you may have to go away for a long time. What would become of Quacky?"

Aunt Maggie had not told the policewoman that Quacky was a runaway from the County Home for Lost Children. She was about to assure her again that her shoplifting days were over, when the front doorbell rang again.

Aunt Maggie went to answer it and saw two men in white overalls on her doorstep. A truck with ladders on it was parked in front of the house and two more men in white overalls stood on the curb.

"Congratulations!" one of the men told Aunt Maggie. "Your house has been chosen to be painted free — inside only — by the Acme Paint Company. It's our annual summer publicity paint-up, free of charge to you. We just want to take pictures, before and after, and use them in an advertising campaign."

"What a rattrap!" another of the painters whispered. "They really picked a tough place this year!"

Before Aunt Maggie could ask Jerry about the painters, they came inside, carrying ladders, drop cloths, cans of paint, and brushes. Immediately, they began setting up scaffolding and moving furniture around while Aunt Maggie and Jerry and Lieutenant O'Rourke watched with their mouths open.

Clem ignored the painters. He was busy trying to explain a double-play on TV to Sumanji and Narguru. It was hard to do, from his chair.

"Miss O'Rourke," Jerry said, turning to her. "If you're not busy this evening, may I take you to a movie?"

"I'm not busy," the policewoman replied, pleased that she had been asked. "I'd like very much to go to a movie with you."

"I'll call you at your office to arrange a time," he said. "But I don't have a car."

"That's all right," she said. "I do. I'll pick *you* up, if you don't think that will be too Women's Lib of me."

"Then you call and pick *me* up." He smiled.

After she left, Quacky came back from talking with Ralph and couldn't believe all the painters in the house.

"Let's get out of here," Jerry told Quacky. "Too many people. We haven't painted Puddle's doghouse yet. How about it?"

They went into the back yard and Quacky chose some bright red paint for the job. He and Jerry talked while they both painted.

"You know, Quacky, I still don't know much about you," Jerry said. "How about telling me more?"

"There's not much more to tell," Quacky said. "All I know about where I came from, Aunt Maggie has told me. My folks left me on the doorstep of a police station in Yonkers. They left a note tied to my diapers saying, 'We love him, but can't keep him. We're flat broke. Give him a name and some love.'"

A lump came to Jerry's throat. "What did the police do with you?"

"They said I squawked as much as a duck, and since the desk sergeant's name was Quackenbush, that's what they called me," Quacky said. "My first name, Wilbur, was given to me later, by the County. That was the name of the first man who filled out a form on me."

"Then what?" Jerry asked.

"Well, the cops at the station in Yonkers wanted to keep me around, like sort of a mascot. But when word got out about me, the County took over. They tried to find my real parents, but they had no luck. Then about a year later, in an orphanage, Aunt Maggie showed up. She said she was my mother's aunt. When they asked where my folks were, she said they both had been killed in an automobile accident."

"Did the police check that out?"

"They did, but they never could prove that the couple that died in the car crash were my folks. So that's about all I know. They wouldn't let Aunt Maggie keep me, because she was shoplifting back then too. So whenever I got the chance, I ran away from orphanages and foster homes and came back here to Aunt Maggie's until someone would come for me."

"Then you're expecting to be caught too, and taken away," Jerry said.

Quacky laughed. "It doesn't matter, about me. I'll find a way to come back here again, if they come for me. Maybe they'll get tired of tracking me down and moving me around.

Maybe they'll finally let me stay with Aunt Maggie."

"And you still might breed pedigree dogs, like you want to," Jerry reminded him. "I've got to figure out a way for you to get the money you need."

"Now tell me more about you," Quacky asked.

"Nothing much to tell," Jerry said. "I've been on the road since I was about sixteen. My folks fought like cats and dogs. I came from a big family, so I figured no one would miss me and I took off. I worked odd jobs for a couple of years and when I was eighteen I joined the Navy. They sent me out to the Pacific, and I sure liked lying on the beaches of all those islands out there."

"What job did you have in the Navy?" Quacky asked. "Was there a war on?"

"I was just a kid, so they had me in charge of the ship's laundry. I made out real good, because all the officers gave me special treatment if I ironed their uniforms extra good. And the mess-hall cook would stuff me with homemade ice cream, in trade for special ironing I did for him. But no war was on. World War Two had ended and we weren't into the Korean War yet."

"Did you like being in the Navy?"

"Oh, it was okay," Jerry said. "Sometimes I'd have fun. We all played poker and dice and I usually won a lot of money. But I'd spend it fast. Or when I was on shore leave in Tokyo or Manila, someone would knock me on the head and roll me and take all my money. Then I'd wake up again aboard ship and be sorry I ever left it. I finally decided that was no way to live. So when my last hitch was up, I got out of the Navy."

"And you kept drifting," Quacky remarked.

"I guess I'm not the sort to ever settle down," Jerry told him. "Aunt Maggie says I'm a typical Gemini — a drifter. And I feel sort of like a caged animal when I think of settling down and staying in one place too long. Or if I think of getting married and having a family. Aunt Maggie says I'll turn out all right, but I have my doubts."

"Did you ever come close to getting married?"

"Twice," Jerry said. "Once, while I was in the Navy. But I left the girl all the money I had instead and took off. Glad I did too! The second time was about three years ago. Boy, I came close that time! I nearly married a lady bus driver. I was driving a bus in Madison,

Wisconsin, and met her at the bus drivers' picnic. She got her hooks into me so deep, I agreed to marry her, but at the last minute I got scared. I left her waiting at the church and made my getaway in my bus! I drove it ten miles out of town before I left it on a side road and hitched my way across four states. I figured I might be safe, that far away from her!"

"Did she ever find you?" Quacky asked.

"No, I moved too much for her to catch up with me. I guess what made me duck out on her was the thought of becoming a father. I knew that once we got married, it probably wouldn't be long. And I guess I've always figured I'd make a good husband but a rotten father."

"Why so?"

"Kids don't realize what an awful responsibility it is, to be a father," Jerry replied. "It means you've got to settle down and maybe keep a job you really don't like. You've got to work at whatever is steady and pays the most. And you have to help raise a kid. You can't leave it all to the mother. Some men are just not up to all that, and I guess I'm one of them."

Quacky had a sinking feeling inside him.

He had been working himself up about Jerry, imagining him as his father. But Jerry had robbed a bank, and if the police were after him, he might have to leave Aunt Maggie's any day and be on the run again. He was hoping Jerry would take him along. Now he was more afraid than ever that Jerry wouldn't.

Aunt Maggie came out the back door, waving her hands excitedly. She looked more upset than Quacky had seen her in years.

"Hide!" she called in a stage whisper to Quacky. "They're here for you!"

Quacky dropped his paintbrush. He grabbed his bicycle and escaped through the back gate. Jerry went inside the house with Aunt Maggie.

"Some people are here from the County Home, for Quacky!" Aunt Maggie told Jerry. "Help me get rid of them!"

A fat man and woman with black briefcases stood just inside the front door. Painters were working all around them.

"Come into the kitchen, or you'll get paint all over you," Aunt Maggie said.

The couple followed her into the kitchen, where they sat at the table with Aunt Maggie and Jerry.

"We're looking for your nephew, Wilbur Quackenbush," the man told Aunt Maggie.

"We've been told that whenever he runs away, he always comes back here to you in Smedley. And we know all about your shoplifting."

"So we've come to take the boy back to the County Home," the woman added. "Where is he?"

"He isn't here," Aunt Maggie said. "He hasn't been here for months."

"Come now," the man insisted. "We've asked your neighbors and they tell us Wilbur has been back here for several days. Why not just make this as easy and pleasant as possible and turn the boy over to us?"

"There's nothing easy or pleasant about taking a boy away from the person he wants to be with and the place he wants to be," Jerry told them. "Why don't you both just leave the boy alone?"

"Please don't interfere," the lady warned Jerry. "Are you related to the boy?"

"I'm just a friend," Jerry replied. "A good friend. But I . . ."

"Then please stay out of this," the man said.

The man and woman got up from the table. "We'll be back in exactly one hour," the woman told Aunt Maggie. "If Wilbur is not here then, for us to take to the County Home, we will have to arrest you for contributing to the delinquency of a minor, among other things."

"Shoo!" Aunt Maggie told them, getting her broom. "Out of my house, the pair of you! The very idea! Scat!"

She swept them out of the house, then went back inside to Jerry.

"They're going to take him away again!" She was sobbing.

"Not if I can help it!" Jerry told her. "Now you just pull yourself together. I'll take care of this."

Jerry left the house by the back door. He looked around for any sign of the social workers who had come for Quacky, but they had driven off in their car. When he was sure it was safe, he went out into the alley and looked for Quacky.

"Here I am," Quacky called down from a window above an old garage a few yards away. "Have they gone?"

"Yes, but they're coming back in an hour, to take you away. Come on down, and we'll talk about it."

They sat inside the empty garage and talked. Quacky was very worried about being taken away. He didn't want to leave Aunt Maggie and was afraid he might never see

Jerry again. And Jerry was beginning to fear that he might never see Quacky again.

"Why don't you and Clem go now," Quacky suggested. "And take me with you? I could be a lot of help."

"If I went," Jerry said, "I'd like to take you along, but I doubt it would be a good idea. Either for us or for Clem. He wouldn't let me take you. Besides having the cops after us for the bank robbery, we'd have the social workers after us. They'd be trying to find you to take you back."

"I could hide," Quacky told him. "No one would see me, if I kept myself hidden under some coats on the back seat of a car. You and Clem have plenty of money now. You could buy a car and make your getaway."

"I've been afraid that I'd be a bad influence on you," Jerry said. "I see now that I have been. Quacky, what Clem and I did was wrong. We held up a bank! Now you think it's okay to get away with it. You'd even help us."

"But . . ." Quacky hadn't wanted to say what else he had on his mind. Now he had to. It was his last chance to get Jerry to change his mind. "But don't you want me?" Quacky looked in Jerry's eyes.

Jerry did not want to hurt Quacky. But

deep down, he knew he would be bad for Quacky.

"I just can't take you with me," Jerry said.

"You don't want me." Quacky looked straight into Jerry's eyes again. But Jerry made himself as cold and uncaring as he could.

Quacky turned away and started out of the garage. He looked as if he were going to cry.

"Quacky, I do want you," Jerry called after him. "I just can't take you with me. I'd be bad for you."

Quacky left the garage and got on his bike. He pedaled away down the alley until Jerry could not see him anymore.

Jerry went back to the house and told Aunt Maggie.

"He'll take off somewhere, probably for a couple of days," she told Jerry. "Until he figures the social workers are gone and won't come back. They may not come back, either, after I tell them he was here but took off again. Thank heavens he can look after himself."

"I didn't mean to hurt him," Jerry explained. "There was no other way. I had to make him think I didn't want him, at least not enough to take him with me. I *would* be bad for him, Aunt Maggie. I'm wanted by the police! I'd better go now. Before I cause any more trouble. Clem and I will leave right away."

"Don't leave just yet," Aunt Maggie told him. "You need to be rested and clear-headed, to figure out where to go next and how to get there. Besides, Quacky may think things out and come back sooner than we think. He may understand why you couldn't take him with you."

"We'll leave tomorrow, then," Jerry agreed. "I do need time to think things over."

"Besides, you promised Lieutenant O'Rourke you'd take her to the movies tonight," Aunt Maggie reminded him. "It wouldn't be kind to run out on her."

Jerry remembered what Quacky had told him about Otis walking out on Aunt Maggie during a movie and never coming back.

"No, I wouldn't do that to any lady," Jerry told her.

"Then, that's settled." Aunt Maggie sounded relieved. "And after the movie, why don't you take Miss O'Rourke to Kelly's Bowling Alley?"

"I don't think I'll be much in the mood for bowling," Jerry replied.

"Oh, you don't have to bowl. You can sit in the cocktail lounge and hear me sing!"

"What?" Jerry asked.

Aunt Maggie strummed an imaginary guitar. "I sing a mean folk song," she explained. "Friday and Saturday nights at Kelly's. They don't pay me much, but it keeps my voice in shape."

"We'll be there," Jerry assured her.

The social workers returned when the hour was up, but Aunt Maggie told them Quacky had gone. She held out her wrists, saying they could handcuff her and take to jail, if they wanted, for contributing to the delinquency of a minor.

They looked at the white-haired old lady with a strong tint of blue in her hair and her frail body and wrinkled face.

"Well, we won't press the matter this time," the man said.

"But if he comes back here, you'd better tell the local police," the woman told her. "They'll get in touch with us in New York, and we'll be back out here for the boy."

"I'll do that," Aunt Maggie replied and they left again.

Clem stayed at home, drinking beer and ordering pizzas in. He watched an old gangster movie with James Cagney and Humphrey Bogart as bank robbers.

Jerry took Miss O'Rourke to see a rerun of two old Dean Martin and Jerry Lewis movies. Miss O'Rourke laughed many times during the double feature, but his mind was on so many other things, he hardly paid any attention to the screen. He wondered where Quacky had pedaled to, and what he was doing.

He was glad when the second movie was over and he could take Miss O'Rourke to Kelly's Bowling Alley.

"A hundred pennies for your thoughts," she said in the car.

"Oh, nothing very serious," he said, trying to shake himself out of it. "Just wondering about how long to stay in Smedley, I guess. Have to find work somewhere. I'll probably go back to Chicago pretty soon."

"Is there someone waiting for you in Chicago?"

He looked at her and saw that she was really interested. Would she be jealous if he had a girl friend to go back to in Chicago?

"No," he said. "I didn't leave anyone behind in Chicago."

Jerry's spirits picked up at Kelly's Bowling

Alley. He and Miss O'Rourke took a small table near the stage in the crowded, dimly lit lounge. After they were sipping their drinks, a yellow spotlight focused on some curtains. From behind them stepped a tall, thin old lady with blue hair, dressed in a long pink gown with purple feathers all over it. She was working hard with a Chinese fan that she kept close to her face, as if hiding behind it.

The audience gave her a big hand and she waited for them to stop clapping before she began. A man at a piano started tickling the keys, running up and down the keyboard. Then he played a lively little melody and Aunt Maggie began her first song.

The crowd began cheering and clapping. The song must have been one of their favorites, but Jerry had never heard it before.

Aunt Maggie brought the house down with that one. Then she belted out a very rousing "Wabash Cannonball." She followed that with a song she said she picked up in a saloon in Chicago years ago, called "Clark Street Mary." It was about a woman named Mary who sang songs in cafés for her supper and for her bottle of wine.

Miss O'Rourke drove both Jerry and Aunt Maggie home after the show and said she couldn't get over how much she enjoyed Aunt Maggie's singing.

"You could be on Johnny Carson's show," Miss O'Rourke told her.

"I'd rather be at Kelly's two nights a week," Aunt Maggie said. "I'd be terribly embarrassed if too many people saw me or heard me sing."

When they got home and Miss O'Rourke had left, Clem told them that Quacky had been back.

"But he didn't stay more than five minutes," Clem said. "He waited until he saw you were all gone. Then he came to say good-bye to Puddles."

"Did he take the pup with him?" Aunt Maggie asked.

"No," Clem replied. "He just played with the dog. He told him he couldn't count on being able to feed both of them, on the run. I tried giving him some money, but he wouldn't take any."

"Did he say anything about me?" Jerry asked.

"No, but he did leave a message for Aunt Maggie. He said, 'Tell Aunt Maggie not to worry and I'll be home in a couple of weeks or a couple of months.'"

Aunt Maggie started crying again and Jerry comforted her. He got them all some beer and they sat around the kitchen table and talked and drank for hours. Jerry kept insisting that he should go out and look for Quacky. But Aunt Maggie convinced him that that would be too dangerous for him and Clem. Quacky had taken care of himself before, she said. He would do it again.

"He'll be back, or do okay," she told them. "Wherever he goes. He's an Aries. He'll land on his feet."

But Jerry was worried about him.

It began to thunder and then rain hard. Aunt Maggie called Puddles in from his dog-house and let him sleep in the kitchen.

While the rest of the house was asleep, early in the morning while the sun was just coming up, Puddles left the kitchen. He made his way upstairs to Quacky's bedroom and sniffed around the two mattresses where Jerry and Clem were sleeping. He didn't find Quacky sleeping in his usual place, in the middle, so he sniffed around the floor.

After exploring shoes and socks, Puddles became intrigued with a cold, hard something near Jerry's mattress. He put his paws on the thing, and to his surprise, whatever it was opened up and things were inside.

The things had no smell, but they felt good to touch. He felt around with his one white paw. There were some objects, but he didn't know what they were. He took one of them up in his paws and began licking it. It didn't taste like anything good to eat, so he tried chewing on it. He thought it would be fun to tear it apart. But it was very hard, so he didn't get anywhere chewing on it.

It became more and more interesting to him, though. He took it into his mouth and went downstairs with it to the kitchen. There he played with it a while longer, then hid it under one of the cabinets. Afterward, he went back upstairs and crawled under the sheet where Quacky had always slept.

Later that morning, the rain stopped. While Aunt Maggie began making breakfast, Puddles went out the back door and into the yard. It was his own secret that he had taken a new plaything with him. He took it out to his dog-house and played with it until Aunt Maggie came out with his breakfast.

When she went back inside, Puddles occupied himself again with his new plaything. Later, when she came out to take the garbage to the alley, she accidentally left the back yard gate partly open before going back inside the house.

Puddles took his new-found toy and walked to the gate, to explore. Pushing his nose against it, he found that the gate opened. He discovered marvelous smells out beyond.

Soon he was out into the alley. That led him farther from the back yard to the end of the block.

He would let go of his new plaything for a few minutes, to sniff around and chew on new things he found. Then he would go back and pick up his toy and carry it farther down the alley.

This was fun for Puddles. Exploring. And he had this nice thing to take with him.

THIEVES FALL OUT

"Clem's ankle feels better and he wants to go," Jerry announced to Aunt Maggie after breakfast. "But I've made up my mind to go looking for Quacky. Tell Clem I'll be back when I'm back. And for him not to get any funny ideas and run off with the money or the toy collection."

"I wouldn't trust him," Aunt Maggie said. "I'd take half the money and half the toy collection with me, if I were you."

"That'd be a lot of money to carry around," Jerry replied.

"Better than taking a chance on coming back and finding Clem gone with all the money and the toys."

While Jerry went upstairs for his half of the money, the painters returned. In minutes they were climbing all over the scaffolding and dripping paint again. Clem was trying to explain a foul ball to Sumanji and Narguru, who kept clanging their finger cymbals while he went through sign language for them.

Jerry took fifty thousand dollars in hundred-dollar bills out of a big envelope in a drawer where he had hidden it and stuffed it into his pockets. Then he felt around under his mattress for the metal box.

It wasn't where he thought it ought to be, at the head of his mattress. He reached around the whole mattress and finally flipped the whole thing over, frantically looking for the box.

After a few minutes he ran down the stairs fast. He almost tripped down the last half dozen steps.

"The box is gone!" he shouted to Clem.

Clem leaped out of his chair, forgetting his still-sore ankle. The two missionaries looked at them, still clanging their cymbals. One of the painters, high on a ladder painting trim around the living room ceiling, became startled. He spilled a bucket of yellow paint that landed on top of the television set. Yellow painted poured down over the screen.

"The kid got it!" Clem shouted. "We've got to get the kid!"

Jerry ran out the front door and Clem hobbled after him as best he could.

Aunt Maggie watched them from the door as they left, holding her hands up to her cheeks. Where had Quacky taken the box, she wondered. And what would happen next?

"Well," she said, returning to the living room and the mess the painters had made. "Now we finally got a color TV!"

Puddles was not used to crossing streets. No one had taught him to look both ways.

A limousine, black and long and shiny, screeched to a stop just inches away from running over him. A chauffeur and his passenger in the back seat, a distinguished-looking old man in a black suit, got out and went to the front of the car.

"Poor little mutt, he's frightened," the chauffeur said, picking Puddles up.

"What's he holding on to?" the man in the suit asked. "Let me see."

The chauffeur took a small metal object out of Puddles's mouth and handed it to his employer.

"It looks like a toy soldier," the chauffeur said. "A mechanical bugler."

"This is part of . . ." The old man stopped himself. "Whose dog is this?"

"There are some tags around its neck," said the chauffeur, "but no name tag."

"Puddles!" a young voice called out.

The chauffeur and the old man turned to see a lanky boy in a blue football jersey and old blue jeans running toward them. He looked very excited about something.

"That's my dog!"

"Young man, your pup is fine," the old man said. "But I must ask . . . where did he get the object he was holding when we picked him up?"

Quacky looked at the object and realized it was the toy bugler from the collection Jerry and Clem had stolen.

"I've never seen it before, sir," Quacky told him. "He must have picked it up in some alley. He wandered off from our house some hours ago."

The old man took Quacky aside so his chauffeur could not overhear him. He gave Puddles back to Quacky but kept the toy bugler.

"This is part of a collection stolen from my bank," the man said. "I am Chester MacDougall, president of the Smedley First National Bank. The collection belongs to . . . the bank. Do you know where the rest of the toys are?"

Quacky crossed his fingers behind him and replied he didn't have the foggiest idea where the other toys were. Or if there were others. Or how Puddles got hold of the one.

"I think it would be a good idea if you and your pup took a ride with me back to my bank," said Mr. MacDougall. "I'd like to talk to you further about this in the privacy of my office."

Later, in the bank president's office, Quacky sat on one side of a large desk with Puddles in his lap. Mr. MacDougall sat behind the desk and they were alone in the room.

"You insist you don't know where the rest of the toy soldiers are," Mr. MacDougall probed, looking closely at Quacky.

"Never saw even this one before," Quacky repeated.

The bank president took a checkbook from his inside suit coat pocket. Quacky watched as he made out a check for two thousand dollars.

"It's yours." Mr. MacDougall pushed the check across the desk at Quacky. "No questions asked. If you return the rest of the collection."

"No questions asked?" Quacky wasn't sure he heard right.

"That's correct." Mr. MacDougall nodded. "All I've left off this check is a name. To whom shall I make it out?"

Quacky thought hard. Finally he sat back in the big chair and petted Puddles.

"You can make it out to my aunt, Maggie Silversmith." The name sounded odd to Quacky. He hadn't thought of her last name for a long time. "But she didn't take your collection and she didn't rob your bank! *I* found the toys, in a garbage can!" Quacky crossed his fingers again.

"I'm not interested in any of that," Mr. MacDougall said. " 'No questions asked,' remember? But you don't get the check until you return all the toys to me. Here in this office, within an hour."

"And no questions asked?" Quacky reminded him. "Like you promised? You won't call the police?"

"I promise," Mr. MacDougall assured him. "I don't want publicity on this any more than you apparently do. My board of directors of the bank just wouldn't understand, about my hobby. But to explain to you. . . . When I was a boy, even younger than you . . . I saw a toy soldier. A bugler just like the one your dog so kindly gave up to me. And like this one, he could actually play a tune. But I was very poor

154

and couldn't afford to buy it. All my life, as I became rich, I wanted to have not only that toy bugler, but a whole army of miniature mechanical soldiers. Ten years ago, I began collecting them and now I must have one of the finest toy-soldier collections in the world."

"I hope Puddles didn't chew too hard on your bugler," Quacky said.

"It can be repainted." Mr. MacDougall wasn't too worried. "No serious harm done. I'm just ever so glad he chose one of my toy soldiers to play with on his roving. I'll be waiting for you to return the rest of them. No questions asked, I promise."

Quacky left with Puddles and kept looking behind him, to see if he was being followed. He had a strong hunch that someone was on his trail.

When he got back to Aunt Maggie's house, he found Jerry and Clem gone.

Aunt Maggie gave a sigh of relief. "They're out looking for you!" she told him.

Clem came hobbling in through the front door just then, before Aunt Maggie could ask Quacky about the missing box of toy soldiers. When he saw Quacky, he started for him.

"Where are those toy soldiers?" Clem demanded angrily. He grabbed Quacky by the front of his football jersey.

"I don't know." Quacky squirmed to free himself. "I suppose wherever you put it." He thought it wise not to tell Clem anything, especially about his arrangement with Mr. MacDougall. He wanted to tell Aunt Maggie, but how could he, with Clem holding him?

"Jerry looked upstairs by his mattress where he kept the box of toys," Clem said. "But the box and the toys weren't there. There's only one person who could have taken them and I'm lookin' at him!"

"It must be still upstairs," Quacky insisted. "Maybe you didn't look good enough. Maybe one of the painters moved it, or took it."

Clem looked as if he didn't swallow that.

"We'll *all* go look upstairs," Clem told Quacky and Aunt Maggie. They looked high and low, but couldn't find the metal box.

"Maybe Sumanji or Narguru took the box," Aunt Maggie suggested.

Clem checked that out by going up to the attic and searching the missionaries and their few things.

While he was upstairs, Lieutenant O'Rourke came to the front door and Aunt Maggie let her in.

"I've been worried about Jerry," she told Aunt Maggie. "I thought he might go back to Chicago without saying good-bye."

"He's gone on some errands," Aunt Maggie said. "I don't expect him back for a few hours."

"Oh, is this your nephew?" Miss O'Rourke asked. "You must be Quacky."

Quacky shook hands with her. He was glad she was here. Now maybe Clem couldn't make any trouble for them.

"Aunt Maggie, it's about lunchtime," Quacky told her. "Maybe Miss O'Rourke would stay and have lunch with us?"

Aunt Maggie quickly caught Quacky's meaning and invited Miss O'Rourke to stay. She agreed and they were out in the kitchen when Clem called Aunt Maggie out of the room.

He whispered to her, "I think maybe Jerry took it! And if my hunch is right, he took his half of the stolen money too." Clem pointed his gun at her. "Now come with me upstairs while I look."

Clem searched the drawer where he and Jerry had kept their money. He counted the bills and turned to Aunt Maggie.

"Half of it's missing! No. More than half — we spent some!" He looked pale. "Jerry's left with more than his share of the money and the whole toy collection!"

"But we saw him leave the house," she

protested. "And he didn't have the metal box with him."

"Then he hid it somewhere and he's gonna come back for it," Clem said. "But I'll make sure he don't run out on me, and that he don't collect the reward money for himself."

Clem held his gun on Aunt Maggie. "If that kid is in on this with Jerry," Clem said, "it's too bad for him and you. Now get rid of that lady cop downstairs. I don't care how, but get rid of her!"

While Aunt Maggie was upstairs with Clem, Quacky excused himself from Miss O'Rourke. He took Puddles out the back door and into the yard. He got on his knees in front of the doghouse and felt around inside it.

"Just where I left it," Quacky said, relieved. He took out the metal box and then ran for all he was worth to his bicycle. In seconds he was pedaling hard, away from the house, with Puddles and the metal box in the wicker basket on his handlebars.

I know you can handle Clem, Aunt Maggie, Quacky thought as he pedaled. Just hang in there, until I come back!

Quacky made it back to the bank president's office with Puddles just before the hour was up. He handed the box over to Mr. MacDougall and the bank president handed him the check for two thousand dollars.

"Now, young man," Mr. MacDougall said, "you wouldn't also happen to know where the stolen hundred thousand dollars is, would you?"

"I only found the toys," Quacky replied quickly. And that, at least, was true. "I don't know anything about any stolen money. Can I go now?"

"Yes," Mr. MacDougall said. "But promise not to say a word about the toy collection to anyone?"

"If you won't tell anyone I found it," Quacky insisted.

"It's a deal," Mr. MacDougall agreed. "The two-thousand-dollar reward money is a personal check on my own account. I don't have to explain it to anyone. I'll just let the police know I found the collection myself, and that will end the matter."

Quacky left the bank and again checked to see if he was being followed. He didn't see anyone and got on his bicycle with Puddles and pedaled back home.

Quacky heard some brakes shriek. Then someone yelled, "Hey, Quacky, hold up!"

Quacky turned and saw a familiar face.

Jerry was waving to him from a taxicab. He got out of the cab and paid the driver. Then he ran to Quacky.

Quacky almost wanted to ride his bike away, to avoid seeing or talking with Jerry. He really had nothing more to say to Jerry, and he didn't think Jerry had anything more to say to him.

"You've got to let me explain," Jerry pleaded. "I didn't mean what I said yesterday in the garage. I wanted you to come with me, Quacky, I really did. But I still don't think I'd be a very good influence on you. That's why I said no."

Quacky felt a lot better. He wasn't sure whether Jerry was saying he would take him with him after all. But it was enough to know Jerry wanted them to be good friends again.

"I was worried about you," Jerry said. "I know you're able to take care of yourself. But I was still worried. I see you and Puddles are back together."

"I'm more glad you and I are back together," Quacky told him. They shook hands good-buddy style, locking each other's thumbs in their handclasp. "But I've got some explaining for you."

Quacky told the whole story. How Puddles

had taken the toy bugler and the bank president had found it when his limousine had nearly run over Puddles in the street. And how he made a deal with Mr. MacDougall and returned the whole toy collection. He showed Jerry the check for two thousand dollars.

"Then you *did* steal the toys from beside my mattress."

Quacky nodded yes, and looked down.

Jerry looked very disappointed. "You've picked up a bad habit from me."

"I knew you were going to give the toys back," Quacky explained quickly. "But I thought you would never get Clem to agree. I was afraid he would never see it your way. So I sneaked into the house this morning, while you were all asleep, and I took the collection and hid it in the doghouse. I didn't know then that Puddles had already beaten me to the soldiers when he ran off with the bugler."

Jerry laughed. "The doghouse was a good hiding place!" But then he frowned as he looked at the check. "Aunt Maggie's full name is on it. The bank president and police can trace it to her house!"

"I didn't think of that!" Quacky moaned. "Jerry, what have I done?"

"Oh, it's okay, Quacky." Jerry was thoughtful. "I knew I had to be moving on anyway. But now I'm afraid I can't go back to Aunt Maggie's with you. And Clem may be arrested if he stays there. He left with me, when I went looking for you. I don't know if he's still out looking or if he went back to Aunt Maggie's. With that sore ankle of his, he can't have gone far."

Quacky said he was sorry. But he didn't think the bank president would go back on his word and tell where he got the toy collection.

"Maybe so," Jerry said. "But I just can't take the chance. I'd better telephone Clem at Aunt Maggie's and warn him, if he's there. Do you have some change? All I've got are hundred-dollar bills."

Quacky had a couple of dimes and they found a telephone booth on a street corner and called Aunt Maggie's.

Jerry told Clem what had happened. Before he had a chance to go on, Clem yelled, "What's the idea of taking off with more than your share of the money?"

"I've made up my mind to turn myself in and give back the money," Jerry told Clem. "Why don't you too? I don't want to be a bank robber anymore. I want to get back to being a carpenter, even if I only get to work in jail."

"No way," Clem said. "I'm getting out of this house and this town while I can. Know who's here now, snooping around? A cop with skirts! If she gives me any trouble, I'll take care of her. I've still got my gun!"

"You leave her alone!" Jerry warned him. "And Aunt Maggie too. Just blow, if that's what you want. But don't do anything stupid like harming those women!"

"Not unless they give me trouble. So long, pal. Don't hit any knots with your hammer." Clem hung up.

"He's splitting," Jerry told Quacky. "With his half of the money."

"Are you really going to give yourself up?" Quacky asked. "And return your half of the money?"

"Yes. I'm gonna go to old MacDougall now and take my lumps," Jerry said.

"Can I come along?"

"You might as well," Jerry replied. "It's because of you, mainly, that I'm giving myself up. I've got to teach you right from wrong somehow. But you've wanted me to do that all along . . . turn myself in and return the stuff. I want old MacDougall to know that, so you get the reward money. And also to convince him that you've been honest all through this whole thing. You and Aunt Maggie were our prisoners. You had to do what we told you."

Quacky's bike fit in the trunk of the taxicab Jerry hailed and they drove with Puddles to the bank. Mr. MacDougall was in his office and a guard told them he couldn't be disturbed.

When they tried to get past the guard outside Mr. MacDougall's door, they were stopped. Mr. MacDougall heard them outside his door and came out. When he saw Quacky, he told the guards to let him and his friend in. Then he asked the guards to let them alone.

Jerry took out his gun and Mr. MacDougall put his hands up.

"Don't shoot!" he said. "I'll give you whatever you want!"

"I'm not gonna shoot you, Mr. MacDougall," Jerry assured him. He put the gun on the bank president's desk.

Mr. MacDougall quickly grabbed the gun and held it on Jerry.

"No need to worry about anything," Quacky informed the bank president. "He's turning himself in and returning the money."

Mr. MacDougall lowered himself into his chair behind the desk and took out a handkerchief to wipe the perspiration off his forehead.

"I was out of work for six months and broke," Jerry explained.

"Put your hands behind your head," Mr. MacDougall told Jerry, holding the gun on him.

Jerry did as the bank president ordered. "I know now I was all wrong," he said, "robbing the bank. My pal and I only wanted five hundred dollars. But one of your tellers practically gave us the key to the vault. We didn't even know what was in the metal box he shoved in our hands!"

"It was going into the vault," Mr. MacDougall explained. "For safekeeping. I ought to call some guards in here, just in case."

"Jerry won't try anything," Quacky assured Mr. MacDougall. "We wanted to talk to you alone."

Mr. MacDougall looked anxiously at Jerry. "Do you have the money on you?"

"In my pockets." Jerry lowered his hands. He was about to empty his pockets, when Mr. MacDougall got nervous. He waved the gun and told Jerry to keep his hands up.

"You empty his pockets," Mr. MacDougall told Quacky.

Quacky found thick packs of new paper money in each of Jerry's pants pockets. He put all the money on Mr. MacDougall's desk.

"Only half of the hundred thousand is there," Jerry said. "My partner didn't agree with me about giving himself up. He'll get caught sometime, I suppose."

"Sooner than you think," Mr. MacDougall assured him. "I couldn't withhold evidence, when our young friend here returned the toy collection. I've made full reports to the police and told them what the collection is. I'll have to face the public on that. And my board of directors. Don't think people aren't laughing at me already."

"You sent the cops to Aunt Maggie's already?" Jerry asked.

"Your friend Clem has been arrested," Mr. MacDougall revealed. "And his half of the money has been recovered. The stolen hundred thousand dollars is accounted for now, unless you spent any of it."

"About sixty dollars," Jerry admitted. "Just for food and a few beers."

"Well, I'll ask the authorities to go a little easier on you than on Clem," Mr. MacDougall said. "Because you did give yourself up and return your half of the stolen money."

Quacky looked sadly at Jerry. "You're going to go to jail, because of me."

"Because of Puddles, actually," Jerry corrected him. "And because of myself. But you did right, Quacky. You did the only honest and smart thing, returning the toy collection and convincing me to give myself up."

"How long will Jerry have to be in jail?" Quacky asked Mr. MacDougall.

"That will be up to the judge," the bank president replied.

"Don't worry," Jerry told Quacky. "I hear that in jail they give you three meals a day and movies."

"I'll write you," Quacky said. "And come see you, every visitors' day."

"I'd like that." Jerry looked pleased. "Mr. MacDougall, can I lower just one of my hands, for a second?'

"Just don't try anything funny," the bank president warned.

Jerry lowered his right hand and mussed up Quacky's hair on the top of his head affectionately.

"All right, now I have to buzz for the security guards to come and get you," Mr. MacDougall told Jerry.

"Go ahead. I'm ready to take my lumps now."

"By the way," Mr. MacDougall added, "the boy and his aunt will be entitled to the thousand-dollar reward money, for helping us get back the stolen money."

"Hey!" Jerry laughed. He had his hands over his head again as Mr. MacDougall kept the gun on him. "You and Aunt Maggie will be rich, Quacky! Three thousand dollars! What'll you do with all that loot?"

"I think you know." Quacky was smiling.

Jerry did know. It would mean Aunt Maggie wouldn't have to shoplift anymore. Quacky would not have to live in orphanges anymore. And if he still wanted to raise pedigree dogs, he could raise as many as he wanted.

Quacky looked at Mr. MacDougall. "Aunt Maggie and I'll put the money in your bank. In a savings account that draws as much interest as possible. And don't you usually get a toaster or a waffle iron or something, for opening up a new account?"

"You'll make a good bank president someday, young man," Old MacDougall remarked, as the security guards came in to get Jerry.

FUN AND GAMES

Quacky found himself to be an overnight celebrity. Newspaper and television people swarmed all over Aunt Maggie's house to take pictures and interview him.

Aunt Maggie was glad that the house painters had finished. Everything looked so clean and fresh.

Sumanji and Narguru did not understand what all the fuss was about. But the photographers managed to get them into every picture and on television.

More money came Aunt Maggie's way, as her horoscope had predicted. Checks poured in from do-gooders all over, and the editor of the Smedley daily newspaper asked her to write a column on astrology. She was glad to accept. The president of Acme Paint Company came to the house and personally presented her with a check for five hundred dollars, thanking her for all the publicity for his paint. She immediately deposited it in her growing savings account with old MacDougall's bank.

The mayor of Smedley came to the house while television crews were filming. He presented Puddles with a blue ribbon and a trophy and one hundred dollars for his part in breaking the case.

For good measure, the Adelphi Pet Food Company gave Puddles a large trophy and Quacky, his master, a check for three hundred and fifty dollars. They called Puddles "The Dog of the Year."

All the money they received made a total of about eleven thousand dollars and it was good enough to change the County's mind about Aunt Maggie. She was given permission to act as legal guardian for Quacky. They celebrated that by sending out for pizza and beer for Aunt Maggie and Quacky drank a Coke.

"Tomorrow, after I visit Jerry in jail," Quacky announced to everyone after the dog-food people gave him his check, "I'm going to New York to appear on *Mid-Day Fun and*

Games. The last time I was on, I was called an 'undesirable person,' and it was a gas!"

Aunt Maggie looked very proud of him.

"I'm going to be 'Boy Celebrity of the Day'!" Quacky bragged. "Bet I do better than Charles Q. Carlisle did last week. He chickened out and wouldn't go into the lion's cage or ride the greased pole into the water tank."

Since both Jerry and Clem had pleaded guilty, they were swiftly tried by a judge. Clem got five years because he was making a getaway when he was caught. Jerry was sentenced to two years because he had given himself up and returned half of the money.

Quacky took Puddles with him to the prison where Jerry was being held. A considerate guard let him take the pup into the visitors' room with him.

Jerry was happy to see Quacky.

"How are they treating you?" Quacky asked.

"I'm working as a carpenter," Jerry said. "Learning lots. I'll be pretty good when I get out of here."

"Aunt Maggie and I will help you go into business," Quacky told him. "If you want, you could come back to Smedley and live with us. Both Aunt Maggie and I want you to. She said she could use the rent, even though she's got lots of money in the bank now. There are lots of doors that need fixing and things to repair."

Jerry appreciated the offer very much, but said he would think about it.

"Clem too, if he wants," Quacky added, although he still wasn't very fond of Clem.

Jerry shook his head. "Clem's gonna be in a while longer than me, and when he gets out, I doubt he'd go back to Smedley. He didn't like it there as much as I did."

It was time for Quacky to leave. He and Jerry could not shake hands because of a mesh screen separating them. But Quacky promised to write often and visit every time they let Jerry have visitors. He watched sadly as a guard took Jerry away.

On his way out with Puddles, Quacky passed Lieutenant O'Rourke on her way into the visiting room and said hello. He had a hunch that he would be seeing more of her.

The lobby of NCB Television Studios looked just as big and gleamy and impressive as Quacky had remembered it.

He no sooner entered the building than a

man in a yellow jumpsuit, with a black beard and long cigar, ran up to him.

"Wilbur Quackenbush!" the man called out. "You remember me . . . Sebastian Damon, producer of *Mid-Day Fun and Games*?"

"How could I forget?" Quacky replied. "But just call me 'Quacky.'" He was holding Puddles in his arms. "You don't mind me bringing a friend?"

"Not at all!" Sebastian Damon looked skeptically at Puddles, though. "But we're almost late again! Time for our elevator ride."

"Are you sure Uncle Pinky is ready for me?" Quacky asked, feeling his ears pop on the ride up to the seventieth floor.

"You're a celebrity now," the producer explained. "Even bigger than Charlie Carlisle, the boy genius. Uncle Pinky forgets anything, if it means publicity. We expect to have our largest viewing audience yet, because of you!"

Quacky emerged from the elevator dressed, as always, in his blue football jersey and frayed blue jeans and track shoes taped so they wouldn't fall off his feet. This time, no one swarmed over him and took his clothes off and tried to put him into a suit.

"Play the games as you are," Uncle Pinky

told him. He was fatter that ever and wearing his bright pink suit.

"Two seconds to go!" someone called out in the studio. Half a dozen make-up people did last-minute work on Quacky's face with powder puffs and paint. As before, he sneezed half a dozen times. Some of the powder got on Puddles and he began sneezing too.

"One second!"

"Go!"

Curtains parted onstage as they had the first time, and the stagehands held up their cards to tell when the audience should laugh, clap, and cheer.

"Uncle Pinky's got a special guest today," the fat emcee told the hundreds of people in the studio audience and tens of thousands watching at home on television. "The boy who captured two desperate gunmen who held up a bank in his hometown. He and his aunt in Smedley, Connecticut, were held captive, locked in the basement, and fed stale bread and water and were tortured. . . ."

"You're full of hot air!" Quacky told Uncle Pinky so everyone could hear. "They didn't do a mean thing to us!"

Uncle Pinky didn't like having Quacky take the high drama out of his version of their ex-

174

perience. He hurried him into the first bit of fun.

A curtain opened and revealed a high-wire contraption on a circus set.

"My mother was Arabella Quackenbush, the great trapeze artiste," Quacky boasted. "I can walk that tightrope. Just watch me! But first, how much do I get?"

"The usual thousand dollars," Uncle Pinky said. *"If* you win *all* the fun and games."

"Make that *two* thousand, or I'm going home," Quacky threatened.

"Okay, okay, two thousand!" Uncle Pinky agreed. "You've been around robbers too long!" The audience laughed.

Before Quacky started up a ladder leading to the high wire, Uncle Pinky reached out for Puddles.

"I'll take the hound, if you please." He took Puddles out of Quacky's arms. Puddles growled and snapped at Uncle Pinky until Quacky told him it was all right. Then Puddles quieted down as Uncle Pinky held him and Quacky started climbing the ladder. There was a net below, he noticed. Just in case.

When he reached the platform at the top, drums began rolling below and Quacky knew what he would have to do when they stopped.

He would have to walk the tightrope. He found an umbrella up there to help him balance and he opened it.

Just as the drums stopped rolling, Puddles, down below, spotted a cat someone was holding onstage for another part of the show. He leaped out of Uncle Pinky's arms, and Uncle Pinky let out a yell. It threw Quacky off balance. He fell off the tightrope and into the net as the studio audience screamed and gasped.

As Quacky landed in the net, Puddles made a leap for the cat. The cat leaped from the arms of the person holding it and Puddles chased it across the stage and into the aisles. People began jumping out of their seats as the dog and cat ran up one row of seats and down another. Stagehands came running and tried to catch them.

Quacky eased himself down from the net and tried to get Puddles before anyone else. Crossing the stage, he saw the other fun and games that Uncle Pinky had in store for him. Among them was a huge cage with what must have been fifty dogs inside. Nearby stood another cage with all four sides closed. It looked like the cage at the dog pound which was used to take the unwanted dogs away to be put to sleep.

"Oh no they don't!" Quacky shouted. He opened the cage and let all the dogs out. They ran this way and that over the stage and down into the audience, barking and yelping. Two of them began tearing at the legs and seat of Uncle Pinky's pants while others jumped on the stagehands who were trying to get Puddles and the cat.

In the confusion, Quacky found Puddles hiding under a curtain.

"Come on, fellow," he said. "Let's get out of here!"

He scooped up Puddles and ran for the nearest door. As he entered the next room, a woman who was about to be strangled screamed. A dozen dogs followed Quacky and Puddles onto the set of *Killer-Diller*, barking and yelping.

"Get the kid and dogs off the set!" someone shouted.

More dogs followed Quacky and Puddles as they crossed the stage and he opened another door.

The lady chef in her apron dropped a plate of spaghetti she was holding and she jumped onto a chair. The dogs made quick work of her meal-of-the-day as stagehands pursued them.

Quacky entered the newsroom door again,

knocking down another stack of cards standing against a wall.

The dogs had devoured all the food on the tables in the chef's studio. They followed Quacky and Puddles into the newsroom and jumped on desks and began licking the faces of the newsmen. News items went flying in the air.

The weather forecaster somehow had to go on with the program. But he was confused by the uproar. Just before Quacky left with Puddles, he heard, "An unexpected six inches of snow is predicted for the entire East Coast by morning."

Quacky knew full well that the whole area was in the midst of the biggest heat wave of the summer.

JAILHOUSE ROCK

"Dear Jerry," Quacky wrote from his desk at home with Aunt Maggie.

"Maybe you heard about the way things got out of hand again at *Mid-Day Fun and Games*. I had to free those dogs, though. I thought they were going to be put to sleep. But it turned out I was mistaken about that. Someone should have told me.

"Anyway, I bought all of them at five dollars apiece and I'm trying to find homes for them. If you know anyone in jail who wants a nice dog, I've got lots to pick from. How about the warden?

"I've given up on show dogs, though. Puddles has a blue ribbon and a couple of trophies, and that's enough.

"Aunt Maggie still has her bridge club over on Wednesdays. She wants to have them more often, but she's too busy writing her astrology column and answering letters from her readers. And she hasn't taken a thing from the supermarket that she hasn't paid for. But she sure complains to the checkout girl about the high prices!

"Oh yes, Sumanji and Narguru finally left, yesterday. They took their orange sheets and their cymbals with them. But Reverend Du Vall is bringing three more over this afternoon, to stay for two weeks! I wonder what color bed sheets they'll be wearing?

"By the way, I got a job now. I'm working at the bank you robbed. Old MacDougall got me a part-time job as his own office boy. He says someday I'll probably be president of the bank!

"I can't wait to see you again, Jerry. I'll be up there on Saturday. I get your letters regular. When you get out, we'll go swimming again, okay?

"And don't worry about me tying you down. You can be as free as you want. I know we're pals and we always will be. That's good enough for me.

"Pardon my mush, but not so long ago, when I was in New York, they were trying to tell me I was lost. But if I'm lost, how come I found you?"

He signed the letter, "Your Friend Always, Quacky."

"P.S.," he wrote, "Puddles says Hi!"

"Dear Quacky," Jerry wrote from the cot in his jail cell.

"I was watching on TV when you let the dogs loose. You sure had Uncle Pinky on the run, but he deserved it.

"Sure glad to hear you're gonna be president of the bank in a couple of years. I'm gonna need a job when I get out of here. If I'm good, I hear, I could get out in about a year. That's thanks to you, helping me see things straight, by turning myself in.

"I'll take you up on coming back to live with you and Aunt Maggie, when they let me out of here. Clem says no matter when he gets out, he never wants to set foot again in Smedley. You and I are gonna find lots to do when I come back, and I can come and go as I please.

"You're an orphan, Quacky, but thanks for helping *me* find a home."

He signed it, "Your Friend, Too, Jerry."

Quacky put the letter into his pocket and went out to the back yard. Ralph was there. While Puddles ran around with Clemontis Regis, Ralph squatted on the grass with Quacky.

"I think I'm gonna enter Puddles in a dog show," Quacky told him.

"Dog shows only take pedigree dogs, like Clemontis Regis," Ralph pointed out pridefully.

"Then I'll hold my own dog show," Quacky decided. "For mutts! I'll give blue ribbons and trophies for the Best Mutt of each class. And even one special trophy, for the dog that wets the most!"

"That's not fair!" Ralph said. "Puddles will run away with that prize!"

That Saturday night, Aunt Maggie put on a benefit concert at the prison. Jerry and Clem got front-row seats.

While Aunt Maggie was on the stage of the prison movie theater, all done up in her pink dress and purple feathers, with a spotlight on her, Jerry saw her special guests sitting on the stage behind her. There was Quacky, with Puddles in his lap. Beside him was Miss O'Rourke, looking very pretty in a dress, not her policewoman's uniform. Next to her sat Police Chief Dooley, his wife, and Ralph.

An empty chair stood next to Mrs. Dooley. Jerry heard it was for Mrs. Dooley's brother, Argus, from Idaho, whose wife had left him after nearly thirty years. Mrs. Dooley had left a note at home for him, to meet them at Aunt Maggie's show when he arrived that night from Idaho. But he was late and Aunt Maggie had to start the show without him.

Aunt Maggie started to sing. The jailhouse rocked with cheers and whistles and applause.

Quacky held Puddles close as Aunt Maggie went into "Wabash Cannonball." He was looking down at Jerry in the front row and thinking, you poor Gemini. You think you're tied down *now*. Wait until you get out of jail. Between Miss O'Rourke, Aunt Maggie, and me, your drifting days are going to be over!

While Aunt Maggie was singing, a guard came onto the stage and Quacky saw a tall, distinguished-looking man behind him in a nice blue suit.

"Argus!" Mrs. Dooley greeted her brother from Idaho.

But Argus suddenly stopped, startled. He looked at Aunt Maggie in the spotlight. He let out a choked cry which made Aunt Maggie turn around and look at him.

"Otis!" she cried, surprised and happy. She stopped singing and started for him, but Otis, more recently known as Argus, turned and ran. "Stop that man!" she called to the guards. "Otis, come back to me!"

Between the guards and Aunt Maggie, Otis was trapped. He had no way out.

"Hey, Otis!" Aunt Maggie said, smothering him with her long, thin arms and her kisses. "Where's the popcorn?"